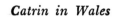

Catrin in Wales

Catrin in Wales

by *Mabel Esther Allan*

Author of *"Swiss Holiday,"*
"Black Forest Summer," etc.

THE VANGUARD PRESS, INC.

New York

Contents

1 – Catrin in Wales – 9

2 – Catrin's promise – 19

3 – Guardian of Gwyncefn – 34

4 – A new friend – 45

5 – The dark young farmer – 57

6 – A shock for Catrin – 72

7 – Protecting the Priory – 86

8 – A disturbing suggestion – 99

9 – Visitors at the Priory – 112

10 – "Welcome to Wales!" – 125

11 – Mystery at the Priory – 142

12 – More mystery – 157

13 – Catrin in danger – 171

14 – The world comes to Wales – 184

15 – Enchanted evening – 194

16 – Catrin looks back – 201

Catrin in Wales

Catrin in Wales

The wind was keen as I struggled to the top of the steep lane and set off along the exposed ridge of the Berwyns. But I had grown very warm during the climb from the valley town of Llangollen and did not mind.

I settled my knapsack into a more comfortable position on my shoulders, tossed back my hair, and tried to walk with the long, steady stride supposed to be common to hill walkers and mountaineers. The trouble was, though, that I was the newest possible hill walker and had never climbed a real mountain in my life. I was far more used to the London streets than to the hill tracks of Wales or any other country.

The sun was shining brilliantly and the hedgerows in the lane I had just left had been covered with half-open hawthorn. It was the third of May and I was in Wales, my mother's country. Wales! I, Catrin Drury, aged just eighteen, was alone and entirely free for the first time ever, with a map in my hand, a few necessities on my back, and the future somehow fluid and unseeable. I did not even know where I would sleep that night. Perhaps Aunt Mair would welcome me with open arms and ask me to stay for a day or two, or perhaps I would go on to the Youth Hostel near Corwen.

It was a strange new experience and one that gave me some satisfaction, though I had had to stifle some cowardly doubts. I had been shy at the Youth Hostel near Llangollen the previous night, for it was my first experience of such places, and the dozen or so other people there had seemed so confident and so much at home in Wales. But I had managed, I hoped, not to seem too much out of things, and I had certainly enjoyed my first contact with adventurous young people.

Until then adventure had been very far from my life. School, then Commercial College, holidays with my family, occasional visits to concerts and theaters. But never, never a lonely road, a knapsack on my back, and a chance to get to know a foreign country. For Wales did seem foreign to me, even though I had heard so much about it from my mother, even though I had been christened the Welsh Catrin instead of Catherine.

My mother had died when I was thirteen, and my father married again the following year. My stepmother was a brisk, attractive woman, and I knew that she made my father happy, but somehow I never managed to get on with her. I had loved my mother passionately and never really got used to seeing someone in her place. My stepmother, whom I called Millicent, was very kind to me, and I think she honestly tried to understand me. It can't have been easy, either, because at fourteen I was shy and self-contained, but with a temper that flared out unexpectedly, frightening me and, I think, Millicent herself.

However, we gradually learned to get on well enough on the surface, and I really tried hard, for my father's sake. But at the back of my mind was always the thought that it would be better if I left home as soon as I was old enough. I thought about it more than ever after my seventeenth birthday, though I knew that in some ways it would be a severe wrench. To leave my father and my little half sister . . . Still, I could see them often, and my father would understand. He was very modern in his views, I knew, and believed in girls' standing on their own feet as soon as they felt capable of it.

As I strode along that high Berwyn track I looked back over the past year, wondering if I would have been happier if I had had any special talent, anything that I longed passionately to achieve.

As it was, I had left my high school just before my seventeenth birthday and had nearly a year's commercial training. I had not enjoyed it much, but it offered a chance of a good job, and independence was what I craved. My training was finished at Easter and then I had a talk with my father, who agreed, a little sadly, that perhaps the time had come for me to leave home. One of my friends, Penelope Grey, already had a good job in an office and was living in a small apartment in Chelsea. She had agreed with enthusiasm to the idea of sharing it with me.

"Yes, Catrin's right to go," Millicent said when the

plans were put before her, and she gave me a slightly humorous, slightly regretful smile. "She's more or less grown up now and isn't without common sense. Penelope's a nice girl and a year or two older, and we can keep an eye on them. But I shall miss you, Catrin. We haven't always seen eye to eye, but still———"

No, we hadn't, but I suddenly knew, with freedom in sight, that I would miss that very downrightness that had been so trying after my mother's dreamy, musical nature. Millicent had been good to me, and it was neither of our faults that we could never quite be at ease together.

So my few possessions went down to the little apartment in a street off the King's Road, and Father gave me a generous present so that I could buy some of the things the apartment would need before it could accommodate a second person. The next thing, of course, was to get a job, but I didn't think there would be much difficulty about that. I had one clear intention before I settled down to being a working woman, and I had been saving up for it for some time. I was going to Wales to see the country my mother had loved so much, and I was going to stay there at least three weeks. My only relative there, so far as I knew, was my mother's eldest sister, Aunt Mair. The rest were dead or far away in other countries.

My father, who had agreed almost easily to my living with Penelope, was not nearly so happy about my intention to set off alone into the blue, but I was determined to go, and Millicent came in on my side.

"Let her go. Yes, I know that awful things happen to people in lonely places sometimes, and I know she's never roughed it. But she's made up her mind, and I believe that Youth Hostels are excellent places, if rather uncomfortable. Besides, she may settle in with this Aunt Mair for most of the time."

"I may not like her, though," I said cautiously, and I had refused to write and announce my arrival. I intended to seek out Aunt Mair without any heralding. She was my mother's sister, but she had been the eldest and my mother the youngest, with almost twenty years between. Aunt Mair must be sixty easily, and I didn't know how long I would want to stay with an old woman in a ruined Priory in the heart of North Wales.

So there I was high on the Berwyns, with a cuckoo calling behind a little fir wood and the Ceiriog Valley just visible on my left. But I was heading for another valley—Nant Gwyncefn—still some miles away, and I was hungry. It was one o'clock and I sat in a sheltered corner near the little wood to eat my sandwiches and fruit, while the lambs cried with a strange sadness all around and the clouds raced over the hills.

How glad I was that I had decided to approach Nant Gwyncefn from above and not by the way of the Dee Valley. The sharp, sweet air seemed the loveliest I had ever breathed, and suddenly, as I set off again, my spirits were very high. Anything seemed possible then, and life was good, though I would have been glad of a companion.

I saw in the distance an occasional solitary cottage or farm, and I could scarcely believe that people spent their whole lives in such a place. Beautiful for a few hours, at most a few weeks, but for a longer period . . . It would be a kind of death.

"What do they *do?*" I asked a pair of lambs with wobbly black legs and quivering black noses. "What do they do at any time, but especially in winter?"

But the lambs had no answer. They shouted wildly for their mother and plunged away over the short-cropped grass.

Oh, yes, I was an utter townswoman, every bit of me, as I walked on toward Nant Gwyncefn.

I met almost no one and presently the fields gave place to bracken and moorland, with here and there deep valleys and wind-blown groups of trees. In the distance were higher blue mountains, with cloud shadows on their slopes. The sun went in and the wind blew very cold indeed, so that I zipped up my scarlet jacket and pulled my gloves out of my pocket.

A glance at the map told me that, if I had read it correctly—and, with the help of the last signpost, I was pretty sure I had—I was only about half a mile or so from the head of Nant Gwyncefn, and soon there should be a track. . . . I sighted it almost at once and strode along it as the sky darkened.

Sharp hailstones sent me flying along toward half a dozen gnarled hawthorns, and, crouching in their inadequate shelter, I pulled my mackintosh out of the straps of my knapsack. Down below me was a deep valley. It looked placid and green after the wild hills through which I had come.

"Quite a shower!" said a voice suddenly at my elbow, and I spun around to see that I had been joined by a dark young man. He wore breeches and leggings and a heavy tweed jacket, and his thick hair was silvered with hail. He had dark eyes and the high cheekbones and unmistakable bone structure of the Welshman. I knew it already, even after only two days in Wales.

"Yes," I said, fastening the last button of my mackintosh.

"You're on a walking holiday, perhaps?" he asked after quite a long pause, while the hail beat over us.

"Yes," I said again. "I'm going to the Priory down in Nant Gwyncefn."

He waved a strong brown hand.

"That's it. Now the leaves are thickening, it's partly hidden, but you can see the top of the central tower and the wall of the chapter house with that high window. A rose window, I believe they call it." His voice was delightful, I thought, with a lilt that reminded me of my mother.

"Is it all in ruins?" I asked, for I had been very puzzled to know just where Aunt Mair lived.

"No, indeed. Part of the Prior's lodging was turned into a house many years ago."

Then the hail fell even faster and more painfully and the wind howled over the hills. For several minutes we were too much occupied in crouching away from the sudden storm to talk, and I had the impression that my unexpected companion was glad.

But when it was over and the sun began to shine brilliantly again he still stood there for a moment, looking down into the valley at our feet.

"It's beautiful," I said, "but so lonely." Then, fool that I was, brash and inexperienced and tactless, I spoke my thoughts aloud: "I just don't see how people can bear it, all the year round. One might as well be dead as live so far from everything that matters."

He stiffened, and his dark glance was suddenly filled with sardonic amusement.

"Some of us," he said quietly, "think ourselves alive enough. Perhaps more alive, indeed, than those who live in cities." Then he nodded and strode away in the direction from which I had come, and I was left feeling small and silly and, unreasonably, half hating him. How dare he laugh at me? If he had always lived in the country, how could he *know* what city people were like?

The world was bright again and the Gwyncefn Valley sparkled under its covering of melting hail. I looked down into it, not knowing that I was hovering between the past and the future, with not the slightest sign that that was the point of no return.

I looked at the Priory buildings through the trees and then at the few lonely farms on the opposite slopes and at what seemed to be a tiny village about a mile from the Priory. The ruins were nearly at the head of the valley, which ended, surprisingly, in a curious gray-white wall of limestone—one of the outcrops that I learned later were not uncommon in that country. Nant Gwyncefn meant the Valley of the White Ridge—though I did not know it then.

I took off my mackintosh and, swinging it in my hand so that it would dry, set off down the narrow, rough lane. The deep banks were creamy with late primroses and with the delicate white flowers of wood sorrel and wood anemones, and every leaf quivered silver.

I could see the little River Collwyn hurrying on its way to join the Dee, and as I reached the floor of the valley I saw two dark little boys playing in the brown shallows.

They glanced at me with bright-eyed curiosity and I smiled shyly, for I was ill at ease with country children. They certainly didn't look "dead"; they looked absolutely brimming with life and naughtiness.

I turned to the left along the only slightly better track that seemed to approach the Priory, and I began to feel a little apprehensive. What on earth would Aunt Mair be like, living alone in this remote place? And yet she *was* my mother's sister, and could perhaps help me to revive my fading memories of her. There might be a likeness, something in the voice . . .

I came presently to what seemed to be the first of the Priory buildings—a building that might once have been a gatehouse, though now it seemed to be used as a barn. Beside it a footpath struck across a field, and it seemed a quicker way than the curve of the road. The grass was soaking wet, but I was wearing heavy walking shoes and did not mind.

Soon I could see the Priory much better, and it looked very impressive against the sharp pale cliff that ended the valley. I seemed to be looking at the whole length of the ruined church. There was a row of pointed arches and part of the central tower. At the western end of the nave were two more towers, one roofless and the other, apparently, whole. I knew almost nothing then about monastic ruins, but I was awed by the grandeur of the pillars and soaring arches.

After all, the footpath did not save me much walking, for it wound around to the eastern end of the ruins and brought me back to the road again, close to a great gateway in a high wall.

A cuckoo was calling nearby, but there were few other sounds and I felt that I had the place entirely to myself.

Very slowly I walked under the gateway arch and found myself on a green lawn—the cloister garth, as I learned later. I drew in my breath sharply, for the dark young farmer had told me correctly. On the west side of the grass, and somehow absolutely part of the ruins, was an incredibly ancient-looking house. It was built of gray stone, and the roof was so thickly covered with bright green moss that the slates or tiles were almost invisible. The windows were mullioned and creepers hung down over the thick old door, which had an old-fashioned bell rope.

Two black cats and a very small kitten were sunning themselves on a dry stone under the overhang of a wall. But when I tried to make friends with them they all moved away.

I stood looking at the bell rope.

"Well, go on! Pull it, you idiot!" I told myself. But somehow I was reluctant to ring that bell and bring my unknown aunt to the door.

However, after a minute or two I did pull the rope and I heard the bell jangling somewhere within. A dog barked, then footsteps approached.

The door opened slowly and I was confronted by an elderly woman with my mother's eyes.

Catrin's promise

I don't mean to sound sentimental, but somehow I immediately remembered my mother's face very clearly because of those dark-blue, rather dreamy eyes. In no other respect, except, perhaps, in the soft singsong of her voice, was Aunt Mair Davies in the least like my pretty mother. She was plump and white-haired, with a rather high color, and she wore an old-fashioned blue cotton apron over a neat dark dress.

She stared at me for a moment and then smiled. It was a nice welcoming smile, as though she liked young people.

"Good afternoon," she said. "You want to see the Priory? Don't mind the dog. Dai won't hurt you." He was a handsome black and white Welsh collie.

"Well, I should like to see the Priory later, perhaps," I said. "But I've really come to see you. I'm Catrin Drury."

My aunt's color deepened and her eyes flew wide open.

"Catrin Drury! My niece Catrin? Oh, my dear! But why didn't you let me know you were coming?"

"I wanted it to be a surprise," I said, not entirely truthfully. How could I tell her that I had wanted, first of all, to make sure that we would get on. A letter might have committed me to a long stay.

"And it is, indeed! A great surprise! Just fancy!" She stared at me almost hungrily. "You're very like Gwynydd when she was your age. I've often wanted to see you, but I rarely leave this valley, and I never thought they'd let you come all this way alone. But now you're almost grown up——"

"Yes," I said. "I'm going to share an apartment with a friend and get a job, but first I'm seeing Wales."

"And so you ought," she agreed. "There's no country like Wales. But come in. Don't stand there on the doorstep. Only do be careful. It's dark after the sunlight. I'm used to all the narrow steps and awkward corners——"

She turned and led the way, and it certainly was dark. I came up against an unexpected angle of the wall and then nearly measured my length down a flight of stone steps that seemed to spiral down into cellars. They spiraled upwards, too, and Aunt Mair, grabbing my arm just in time, said:

"The cellarium of the Priory is down there. Such a useful place for keeping food cool in all weathers. And the other steps lead up to the tower. I've three rooms there where I sometimes put people up."

"You mean they sleep in the tower?" I gasped.

"Oh, yes. It's very comfortable once you get used to the steps. But I sleep in the house myself. There now!" And she flung open the door of a cozy, overcrowded sitting room with a long mullioned window that looked out at the big square of grass and the Priory buildings beyond. There was so much heavy old furniture that there was scarcely room to walk.

"I've never seen anything like it!" I couldn't help saying as I reached the window.

She laughed.

"People often say that, but I suppose I'm used to it. It doesn't seem strange to me. I've been here since my husband died ten years ago. I look after the ruins for the Society for the Preservation of Welsh Abbeys and Castles. Show people around and so on, and they allow me to take visitors sometimes, but I don't bother much, as shopping's difficult."

"And cooking," I suggested tentatively.

"Oh, I've a very good oil stove and a good grate in the kitchen. And there's cold running water. We have sanitation, too. You'd never believe it, would you? This house," she said, "mostly dates from the early thirteenth century, though parts of it have been altered and added to. It was the Prior's lodging. It was an Augustinian Priory, you know. But parts of the church and the cellarium are much earlier. Norman. The rest, except the Chapter House, which is mainly Perpendicular, is Early English. But here I am giving you a lecture and you've come to see me, not the ruins!"

"Yes," I said again, a trifle limply, for I was literally staggered at the idea of anyone living alone in such an ancient place. The thought of the Norman cellarium under our feet oppressed me with the feeling of centuries.

And yet, to my astonishing, homely-looking Aunt Mair, it was just somewhere to keep the food cool in a heat wave!

"Well, sit down, my dear child, and I'll make us a cup of tea. It's rather early, but I expect you can do with it, and I've always got the kettle on the boil."

She bustled off, and I remained standing at the window, looking out. I could see sideways into the grassy nave of the church, and the sky was very blue beyond the high arches and round window of the Chapter House.

She came back very quickly with a tray on which were the tea things and a plate of homemade cakes.

"You'll stay, of course? Indeed, you must stay for as long as you can. Where did you sleep last night?"

"At the Youth Hostel near Llangollen," I explained.

"You could have the lowest tower room. It only needs bottles in the bed."

"I'd like to stay for a night or two," I said cautiously, but in my heart I wondered what on earth I should find to do at the Priory. Once one had looked at the ruins . . . How little I knew! Looking back, I find it hard to believe that anyone was ever so totally ignorant and unaware as Catrin Drury from London.

"Of course," my aunt said, pouring out the tea. "And you must tell me all about your father and your stepmother. And—isn't there a little girl?"

"Delphine," I said. "She's three."

"And your stepmother?" Her voice held a note of cautious questioning and I answered honestly:

"Millicent, I call her. She's all right. A good sort, but we don't always get on. She's the very practical kind, and until recently I was a dreamy, queer sort of girl. Of course, now that I'm grown up and ready for a job, it's different. I've learned not to be so silly."

"You took after your mother," she said. *"She* was an odd little thing; always away over the mountains and singing to herself. I'd left home then, but I sometimes went back, and Gwynydd was always the shy, quiet one, but so pretty. You're really very like her."

I felt myself flushing. No one had ever called me pretty, and I thought myself rather plain. I have dark-brown hair that is almost straight, but it hangs in a nice shape when properly cut; dark-blue eyes, and a pale complexion.

After that she talked about her life at the Priory and I soon realized that it never even occurred to her to be lonely. She said there were plenty of people at the farms and cottages in the valley, and then there were the tourists in summer. Quite a number of walkers and motorists found their way to the Priory.

"After all, it's quite famous," she said in her Welsh voice, though there was little actual turn of phrase. "Very like Llanthony Abbey in Monmouthshire, so the books say. Even to the Prior's lodging and one tower being turned into dwellings."

"But at night!" I cried. "And in winter——"

Aunt Mair dismissed both night and winter cheerfully.

"Oh, well, I don't mind. There's always Dai. Wonderful company he is. And then the cats—— Have you seen them? Bledig and Betsi, I call them, and they have such a pretty kitten. You've no idea how beautiful it all looks under snow, and Mr. Jones from the Collwyn Arms would never let me starve. Many's the time he's cut his way through the drifts to bring me my supplies. But I must admit that since I've not been so well I've wished I had someone nearer."

"Aren't you well?" I asked.

"Oh, it's nothing much, but I've been having queer turns—giddy spells and so on. Perhaps it's my eyes. One of these days I'll go and see the doctor. I get about on my bicycle, you know. Very spry on a bicycle, I am, though I was sixty-one my last birthday." And she laughed.

When we had finished the tea and cakes she told me to bring my knapsack to the lowest tower room, and I followed her cautiously, with due respect for stairways and corners. The narrow, winding steps in the tower were easy enough to see, for there were lancet windows every few feet, and suddenly my aunt turned into a small alcove, fumbling with a low wooden door. When it was opened we entered an unexpectedly large bedroom, crowded with massive Victorian furniture. One wall was composed of a great blocked-in arch, and it was filled almost entirely with a huge wardrobe. I wondered weakly how it and the great double bed had ever been carried up the steps. There was a pointed window that looked down into the nave of the church, but it didn't seem to offer an explanation. The wardrobe had never arrived that way!

"You'll be comfortable here," said my aunt casually. "The bed is very good; feathers. I always like a feather mattress. I'm old-fashioned, I dare say, but there it is. Maybe you'll not mind washing in cold water at the tap downstairs, but you can always carry a jug of hot up here. Only mind you don't trip on the steps."

"I'll be careful," I promised, thinking that the Youth

Hostel had been unbelievably civilized compared to Gwyncefn Priory. And yet—it *was* fascinating! Just for a night, or at most two, it would be like something in a book to sleep in a tower, looking out into a church that had been ruined and unused for—how many hundreds of years?

"Henry the Eighth and all that," I told myself vaguely. "The Dissolution of the Monasteries. Fifteen-something-or-other, then." And for a fleeting moment, as we turned to the door, I visualized the church great and splendid, with stained-glass windows and carved choir stalls and black—or would it be white?—robed monks chanting the office at dusk or dawn. Had the last ones known how very soon the building would be despoiled and the grass grow underfoot?

I gave a small, involuntary shiver and my aunt turned around to ask:

"Are you cold? I could put an oil heater up here. The weather's cold for May. The valley's sheltered, but with all that hail——"

"No, I'm not cold," I said, though the tower room had struck me as being rather chilly. "I was thinking—about the monks before the Priory was ruined."

Aunt Mair leaned against the half-open door. She looked like any comfortable elderly housewife and not a bit like the custodian of an ancient building.

"I often think of them. You can't help it when you've got their buildings all around you. There are books here, and I've read them all. It must have been a strange life, but a good one in some ways. Of course, I'm Chapel, like most other people in these parts, but still—— Everyone was Roman Catholic in those days. If you like I'll show you over the Priory now."

"Yes, please," I agreed. "And then, if you wouldn't mind, I'd like to hear about your home—where my mother grew up."

"It was in the Llanberis Pass," she said, beginning to descend the stairs. "Among the real mountains. She'll have told you."

"Yes, but it's beginning to fade. I'd like to hear it again."

She went down the awkward steps very neatly and quickly, and I followed more slowly, getting a good deal of the whitewash from the wall onto my dark skirt. Near the bottom she suddenly made a very odd sound—she was out of sight around a bend—and then there was a frightening clatter and a crash.

My heart seemed literally to stand still, and in that moment something that had seemed a dream turned into a nightmare. I shot around the last corner and saw my aunt lying on the stone floor at the foot of the tower stairs, with her head and one arm projecting over the steep spirals that went down to the cellarium. She was quite motionless, as though she were dead, and the silence of the whole place was suddenly intense.

I suppose I only stood there for a few seconds, but it seemed like hours. Then a low and rather menacing growl brought me to myself. The Welsh collie, Dai, was standing in the far doorway, teeth bared and tail drooping. He came forward very slowly and sniffed at his mistress's white hair as it spread over the top step.

"Good dog!" I said, not at all liking his unfriendliness. Heaven only knew how his mind worked. Perhaps he thought I'd done something to hurt his mistress.

He answered with another growl, his eyes fixed on me. But then he sat down at a little distance and made no further sound as I bent over my aunt. She was breathing; that much was a relief, but I was afraid that she was badly hurt. I did not at all like the position of her left hip and leg. I had learned some first aid at school, and I remembered that people should never be moved if it seemed that bones were broken, but how could I leave her in such a place?

Trembling all over, I went slowly along the dark passages to the sitting room and grabbed a couple of cushions and a thick dark tablecloth. Then, very cautiously, I moved Aunt Mair a little, finding it difficult, as I was rather slight and she was quite a heavy woman. When I could see her face properly I was relieved to see that she did not seem to have injured her forehead in the fall. There was no cut or bump anywhere, but she was deeply unconscious, and help was an immediate necessity.

"Good dog, guard her!" I said to Dai, and wished that I could speak Welsh. My aunt had said that she spoke Welsh more often than English except to visitors, and perhaps he was more used to it.

I fetched my red jacket and zipped it up and then dashed outside, almost braining myself on a low arch a few feet from the front door. In a shed I found a rusty old bicycle, and I was in such desperate haste that I rode it across the grass and through the gateway.

Once on the road I paid no heed to bumps and ruts, but rode like the wind through the brilliant afternoon, scarcely noticing anything.

"Mr. Jones at the inn," I thought, and prayed that there would be a telephone.

I felt sick and my hair was sticking to my forehead when I dismounted outside the little gray building that bore a board: THE COLLWYN ARMS. The village was beyond, and I saw a telephone kiosk outside the tiny general shop and post office. But Mr. Jones was nearer. He was working in the inn garden; a small, rather swarthy man in his shirt sleeves.

"You must be Mr. Jones!" I gasped, leaning over the wall. "I'm—— I was visiting my aunt at the Priory, and she fell coming down the tower stairs. I think she must have had a queer turn; she told me she's been having them lately. I'm afraid she's hurt badly. A broken leg, at least."

Mr. Jones wasted no time. He strode to the gate.

"Well, indeed! What a terrible thing to happen and wassn't I always telling her that she ought not to live there alone? Sit you down, girl, and I'll telephone for the ambulance."

My legs were shaking so much that I was glad to sink down onto the stone bench outside the inn, and Mr. Jones ran down the road to the telephone. He was away only a very short time.

"It's coming they are, and she'll be in the hospital in no time. They'll take her to Wrexham. Now issn't it unlucky, but my wife and daughter are away in the town? A great hand with illness, my wife is. I'll just fetch my old bike and come back with you. Her niece, you say? I wass nefer knowing she had a niece."

"Yes. Catrin Drury from London," I said weakly. "Her youngest sister was my mother."

"Well, fancy that!" And he nodded to himself as he went around the inn, returning in a moment or two with a bicycle nearly as rusty and old as Aunt Mair's.

"Will the ambulance have to come from Wrexham?" I asked as we pedaled along the road. I had got my breath back but still felt rather sick.

"No, indeed. From Llangollen. Don't you worry now, girl, for it will be along in no time."

And he was right, for we had not been back very long before there was the sound of a warning bell up the valley. My heart leaped with thankfulness, for I had hated feeling so helpless. The ambulance attendants greeted Mr. Jones familiarly, and Aunt Mair was lifted with infinite care onto a stretcher.

"Are you coming with her, Miss?" one of the men asked, and I said:

"Yes. Yes, I suppose so. Will it be all right?"

They nodded, and five minutes later I was in the rocking vehicle on my way to Wrexham.

I remember very little of the next hour or two. Aunt Mair was borne away the moment we reached the hospital, and I sat for a long time in a waiting room. I felt utterly unlike myself; in fact, the morning, when I had not even known Gwyncefn, seemed like another life.

People came and went and hospital smells drifted to my nostrils. I tried to read a magazine, but the words meant very little to me. My thoughts went round and round, and my head ached. There was a bruise over my temple where I had come in contact with the stone vaulting. I was almost glad of it, as it seemed my only proof that I had not dreamed the whole thing . . . the hailstorm, my brief meeting with the dark young farmer, the Priory ruins in the sparkling fields, my aunt's accident.

The brightness of the afternoon seemed to have faded for good. The sky was gray and there were frequent flurries of hail. From the waiting-room window it looked more like winter than May, and I most heartily wished myself back in London. I even yearned for Millicent's brisk common sense.

At last a pleasant-faced woman in a white coat came up to me.

"You're Mrs. Davies's niece? You may go and see her now, my dear, but don't stay more than a few minutes. She's conscious, but very poorly."

"She isn't going to die?" I gasped.

"Oh no. But she has a fractured hip and is suffering from shock." She told me how to reach the ward, and I walked the bare corridors dismally, feeling young and unsure of myself. It was the first time I had ever been in a hospital in my life, for when my mother died so suddenly they wouldn't let me see her.

The ward was long and Aunt Mair was in a bed at the far end. I scarcely recognized her, she looked so different. Much smaller and older. She held out her hand to me and clutched my fingers feebly.

"Catrin! I'm so—sorry, when you'd only just come."

"It's all right," I said awkwardly. "And they'll look after you here."

She was silent for several moments, then she said:

"You're going back to the Priory?"

I had scarcely thought about the future, but my few possessions were there.

"Yes," I said, and her fingers seemed to gain strength from my reply.

"I—shall like to think of you there. Take care of it, Catrin. Promise me, dear girl!"

I was appalled.

"But—but, Aunt Mair, I can't! I don't know anything about it, and—and——"

"You'll soon learn," she said very faintly. "And the Society wouldn't like it if it was left uncared for. They are very keen on Gwyncefn Priory, and they might put someone in my place. I always meant to die there."

"You're not going to die anywhere," I said stoutly, but I could hardly hide my utter dismay.

"Promise me you'll stay for a week or two. When— when I feel better I can make some other arrangement. There's an old friend who lives at Llanrwst—— But, meanwhile, there's ten pounds in the silver teapot. Use it. You will, won't you, Catrin?"

Her eyes were wide, and she looked extremely distressed. A nurse approached, shaking her head at me.

"She mustn't talk any more, dear. You'll have to leave her now."

"Promise you'll stay and look after it," Aunt Mair repeated, and there seemed nothing else to do. I gulped and then said:

"Of course I will. Don't worry about anything. I'll stay for a week or two, anyway." And then, somehow, I got myself out of the ward. The almoner, or whoever she was, came hurrying up to me in the entrance hall.

"Do you want to go back to Llangollen, my dear? Because the ambulance has just brought another case, and you can go back in it."

So back I went to Llangollen in the ambulance, and then I set off to walk along the Dee Valley toward Nant Gwyncefn. I was far too tired to contemplate any more hilltop journeys. And, as luck would have it, a woman motorist gave me a lift to the beginning of the valley.

In the gray evening light Nant Gwyncefn looked like the end of the world to me.

"It ought to be called World's End!" I thought, but I had seen on the map earlier in the day that that name was reserved for a place on the north side of the Dee Valley.

The lambs had ceased crying and the cuckoos were silent, too. Only the river made a faint rushing sound as it flowed over the stones not far from the narrow road. I was cold and hungry and horribly frightened by the thought of having to face the Priory all alone. It had been there, as far as I could judge, nearly nine hundred years . . . it was steeped in history, and not entirely peaceful history, either. The thought of the cellarium, of the winding stairs and cold stone walls, made my hair prickle on my scalp. But I told myself that it had looked utterly peaceful in the afternoon sunlight, that it was beautiful and quiet and that the long-ago despoliation didn't matter now. Aunt Mair loved it, and it was cowardly and childish to mind the fall of darkness. I had promised, and that was the end of it.

I met no one, though I passed some scattered cottages. The farms were mostly well back from the road. When I reached Gwyncefn village it, too, was deserted, though the sound of cheerful voices came from the inn. I wondered whether to appeal to Mr. Jones and his wife, but they were probably both busy at that hour of the evening. It sounded like it.

I went past the inn and sat for a moment on a wall, looking back at the comforting bright red of the telephone kiosk. I had promised to telephone home fairly often, and I suddenly longed to be connected to our big, cheerful apartment in Sloane Street. Delphine would be in bed, and my father and Millicent would be watching television.

But equally suddenly I saw that I couldn't possibly tell them what had happened. They would be terrified at the thought of my living alone at the Priory, even with Dai to guard me. They would tell me to leave at once and go to a hotel or at least a Youth Hostel for the night. And I had promised Aunt Mair that I would take care of the Priory for her.

Slowly I walked on toward the head of the valley, and soon I could see the great length of the ruined church across the fields.

Guardian of Gwyncefn

I approached by way of the road, which was arched with trees and rather gloomy. My spirits were at zero and my feet moved more and more slowly. I thought with sharp longing of London's millions going happily about their evening plans. I saw the red buses swinging in dozens around Piccadilly Circus, and would have given anything in the world for the whole noisy, changing pageant of my native city.

"Oh, London!" I said to myself as I emerged from the trees and saw the high wall and the arched gateway of the Priory before me. Beyond was the pale limestone of the valley's end.

When I reached the Priory entrance I saw something that I had not noticed before, and it gave me some relief. There were stout wooden doors that would swing forward to close the entrance, and they were provided with a couple of large bolts. Outside the gate hung a bell rope even thicker and more primitive-looking than the one by the front door. Tentatively I put out my hand to it, and the bell gave a faint clang, disturbing in the silence. But there was no bark from Dai.

I shut and locked the gates and then stood for several moments contemplating my domain. The old house crouched on my left, dark and rather forbidding in the gray evening, and across the cloister garth the remains of the church filled the sky. Dark clouds were drifting beyond the highest scries of narrow arches.

"Dai!" I called, and would have been thankful to see his long, senstive nose and suspicious bright eyes. But the only creature in sight was the huge black cat, Bledig, and he was sitting on a low wall, staring blankly into the distance with his cold green eyes.

"Where are your wife and child?" I asked, venturing to tickle him under his sleek black chin. He gave me a fleeting look, then stretched every graceful inch of his body and stalked off along the wall.

"A nice friendly animal you are, I must say!" I said sarcastically. "You're more like a witch's familiar than anything else." But the idea was an unwelcome one, and I turned to the front door.

It was closed and, on investigation, locked.

"Mr. Jones," I thought, for when I had gone off in the ambulance he had remained behind.

After a few minutes' search I found the key under a stone. It was a huge iron affair and looked as though it, like the house, dated from the thirteenth century.

The door opened with a loud creak and I looked into almost complete darkness. How I yearned for the comforting modernity of electric-light switches as I groped my way along the passage and into the sitting room, where I thought I had seen a candle and matches. Yes, I had been right, and I pounced on them with relief. There was a large brass lamp, also, standing on the immense old sideboard, but I certainly didn't fancy struggling with oil and wicks. Shielding the candle with my hand, and much disliking the plunging shadows, I went back to the front door and shut and locked it.

Now I was secure in my fortress. . . . No, that was mixing metaphors. It had been a religious house and not a castle. At any rate I was shut in with the atmosphere of centuries.

I remembered with vast relief that there was a flash-light in my knapsack, as well as two spare batteries. It would be ten times better than a leaping candle flame. That candle made me feel as though I were acting in an old-fashioned melodrama.

But to get the flash I had to climb the stairs of the tower, and I had a bad moment when I saw movement on the steps above me. It was only the kitten, and it, at least, seemed pleased to see me. It had not, apparently, learned to copy the aloofness of its parents. I tucked it under my arm for company.

My bedroom had quite a large pointed window, and the gray daylight was still flooding in. It was a relief after the intense darkness of the lower passages. But in an hour or two it would start to get dark.

Armed with the flash and followed by the kitten—not knowing its name, I decided to call it Blackie—I found my way to the kitchen, and there I lit three candles against the coming of darkness and found to my delight that the fire only needed coaxing to burst into flames. The kettle was almost on the boil, too.

I was ravenously hungry, as well as cold, so I found bread, butter, a hunk of cheese, and some apples. I felt a little better when I had eaten and drunk three cups of very strong tea, but I liked my situation no better.

I nearly leaped out of my skin when I heard a distant clangor. The bell by the outer gate! Who could be ringing at that hour? But the thought of any sort of company was more than welcome. I unbolted the front door and ran across the cloister garth.

"Who's there?" I called as I struggled with the bolts, and a girl's voice answered—a high, Welsh voice.

"Olwen Jones. I've a message from my father."

I flung open the gates and was confronted with a girl of about my own age or only a little older. She was extremely pretty in a rather hard way, and she was dressed in clothes that seemed much too smart for the country: sheer stockings, a blue suit, and a rather fussy pink blouse. The suit skirt looked far too tight for cycling, but a bicycle was leaning against the wall.

She, too, had looked me over quickly, and I rather felt that she didn't care for what she saw. I probably looked frightful after the anxious hours.

"So *you're* Mrs. Davies's niece?" she said.

"Yes. Catrin Drury—from London," I answered with as much dignity as I could muster. Somehow I didn't take to Olwen Jones, in spite of the fact that I had been longing for company.

"Well, fancy that! You'll find the Priory very different

from London. Some folk say it's haunted. Very superstitious they are in this valley." Her bright eyes scanned my face.

"Oh, really?" I said with difficult casualness.

"I was looking out of the kitchen window when you passed along the road, and my dad isn't liking the thought of your being here alone. 'Go and tell the girl to come and sleep here, Olwen *fach!*' he said to me. So better be getting your things."

I thought of the cheerful voices at the inn with infinite longing, and even Olwen Jones' company would be better than the silence and eeriness of the Priory. But pride, and the memory of my promise, both surged up in my mind. How *could* I confess that I was definitely afraid of sleeping there alone?

So, before I had really thought, my chin had gone up and I was saying quietly:

"Please thank your father. It's very nice of him—and you. But I promised Aunt Mair that I'd stay here, and I'm really perfectly all right."

Olwen carefully arranged her tightly waved hair.

"Oh, well, indeed it's up to you. I wouldn't care for it at all myself."

"Perhaps I can come and see your father in the morning? He may be able to tell me some of the things I need to know."

"Come about dinnertime, then," she said. "He'll be in Chapel earlier. A pillar of the Chapel, my father is."

"How nice," I said weakly. "Well, thank you." She was turning away to the bicycle, and I must admit I was sorry to see her go. "Oh, by the way, the dog seems to have disappeared. I suppose you haven't seen him?"

She paused with one foot on the pedal.

"Oh, he'll be off over the hills. Very wild is Dai." Then she had gone, bumping away over the stony road, and I once more bolted myself into the Priory. It was already beginning to grow dusk.

I went back into the house, bitterly regretting my foolish pride. After all, I had only promised to look after the Priory. I had not promised to spend every single hour there. But it was too late to change my mind.

I puttered about in the kitchen, reluctant to leave the friendly glow of the fire, and as darkness fell my uneasiness grew. The wind was rising and there was a strange hooting sound out in the ruins. I told myself that it was only an owl, and I knew that it was, but I was still uneasy.

After all, it was a sharp change from an apartment in London to a remote Welsh valley. Even a lonely cottage would not have been so bad, but I could not forget the unknown reaches of the Priory ruins.

As the last of the daylight died I was suddenly possessed by panic in a way that I was ashamed to remember afterward. I rushed up to the tower room by flashlight, seized my knapsack and my mackintosh, and bolted down again, keeping to the wider side of the stairs. It suddenly seemed clear to me that pride would have to go. I could *not* endure all the hours of darkness in that place!

But on the doorstep, with the key in my hand, I knew that I could not face with any greater courage the dark lane under the trees. Hopeless townswoman that I was, the country seemed entirely full of menace.

I returned to the kitchen, washed hurriedly, and put on my pajamas. There was a hot-water bottle hanging on a hook, and I filled it from the kettle. Then, clutching its comforting warmth, I climbed the tower steps again, trying to shut out all thoughts of the cellarium below and the unknown rooms above. I shut the door, put a chair against it, and climbed into the double bed. The feathers received me and I realized that I was aching all over with tiredness.

I slept almost at once, and I dreamed wildly for what seemed hours on end. The Priory bell was clanging, clanging, and when I went to the gate there was no one there. But when I turned around the dark young farmer whom I had met above the valley was looking at me mockingly from the middle of the cloister garth. "Very superstitious they are in these parts," he said. "Have you seen any ghosts lately?" And then his face took on an even more amused look. "You're from the town, where people are half dead. You've no right to constitute yourself guardian of the Priory. Anything might happen, indeed it might!"

Then he changed into Aunt Mair, who, clad in black robes, was leading me round and round the ruins, until I suddenly found myself alone in a vast chamber. It had no doors and I was quite closed in, but the roof was open to the sky.

I woke up, hot and shaking, to find that dawn was breaking in streamers of rosy light and a cuckoo was already calling somewhere in the valley.

Then I slept again, dreamlessly, until nearly nine o'clock.

In the brilliant light of morning my panic of the night seemed absurd and I was glad that it could remain my secret. As I dressed I looked down from my tower window into the grass-grown nave and thought how lovely and peaceful it looked. Bledig was washing himself near one of the pillars and Betsi was sunning herself idly on a stone slab that might once have been a tomb. Their sleek black coats shone in the sun.

I flung back the bedclothes so that the bed could air and marched off down the spiral stairs. I unbolted the front door and stepped down onto the cloister garth, feeling the sun warm on my head. And suddenly I heard an imperative bark.

"Dai's come home!" I cried and bounded to the gates.

Dai backed a few steps when he saw me, then sidled past. Obviously puzzled and unhappy, he circled the grass and then disappeared into the house. When I went into the kitchen to tackle the fire he was standing there, nose and tail outstretched, unhappiness in every line of his graceful body.

"She'll come home. She will really," I told him. "And, meanwhile, I wish you'd make friends with me."

But he still backed away from my advances, and I turned to clean out the deep, old-fashioned grate. Fortunately there was wood and coal in a bucket, but by the time I had the fire going I was very dirty and had to wash as best I could in cold water.

While the kettle boiled I looked at the oil stove and decided that, for the moment at least, it was beyond me.

I would make toast when the fire was clear and be content with that.

I decided to explore at once, for a house that was known would surely be less frightening than one that held unseen rooms and corners. Apart from the sitting room there was a large room with a heavy refectory table and a good deal of old-fashioned furniture. It smelled damp, and I thought it seldom used. There were a great many queer alcoves and cupboards, and a narrow, though not spiral, stair led me up to Aunt Mair's bedroom and a couple of other rooms that were crammed with old furniture. After that I climbed the tower, past my own bedroom, and found that the two higher rooms were very like mine. Once again I wondered how the heavy furniture had ever been carried up there.

Last of all I descended the spiral stair to the cellarium, a trifle relieved to find that Dai was going with me. And, after all, it was not very frightening. Some light came in through low windows and I looked with awe at the stone vaulting and the thick supporting pillars. Near the foot of the stairs was a perfectly ordinary refrigerator; a large one that held a cheering supply of food. Cans of soup, beans and fruit, a shoulder of beef, a pound of butter, a few eggs, and various other things. So I wouldn't starve.

Then I remembered the ten pounds in the silver teapot and went in search of it. It stood on the sideboard in the sitting room, and the money was there under a bundle of receipted bills.

"It seems a shame," I said to Dai. "But I may have to use it sooner or later."

Also in the sitting room were piles of booklets that

turned out to be guides to the Priory, a roll of tickets, and a tin box that held some small silver. I realized with a shock that if visitors came I would have to show them over the ruins, and I took one of the booklets with me when I went back to the kitchen to have my late breakfast. A fine Sunday morning in May might easily bring visitors, I supposed, and I opened the book at the plan of the Priory as I buttered my toast.

After all, it was *my* Priory for the time being, and I had to get to know it.

Later, carrying the plan open in my hand, I wandered around, trying to sort it all out. The nave . . . Yes, of course I knew that it was partly Norman. The massive pillars were Norman and several of the arches; the one above the entrance to the south transept was a huge rounded sweep of stone. I stared at it and found that it gave me pleasure with the blue sky above. Then the pointed windows and arches must be Early English.

Where the high altar had been was just smooth grass, but part of the tracery still existed in the great east window.

The sacristy . . . the chapter house . . . remains of the infirmary . . . line of the east cloister . . .

"I shall have learned something about architecture before I've finished," I said to Bledig, who had been stalking behind me.

He opened his green eyes very cynically and then yawned. "A poor custodian of Gwyncefn Priory!" he probably thought.

After that I wrote a note to Millicent, merely saying that I was at the Priory and would probably stay there for a week or two. I felt rather dishonest, but I didn't dare to explain.

Then I powdered my nose, put on some clear bright lipstick that exactly matched my scarlet jacket, and decided that it was time to go along to the village. Surprisingly it was a quarter to twelve. If Mr. Jones were still in Chapel I could telephone to the hospital first to see how Aunt Mair was.

I gave Dai a large bone that had evidently been put aside for him and watched him carry it away into the church. A most unsuitable place for bone eating, but Dai couldn't be expected to realize it!

It really was a heavenly morning, though not very warm. I felt in reasonably high spirits as I cycled along the road, though I still was not in the least reconciled to being tied to the Priory for a couple of weeks. I dreaded the coming of another night, but just then it was impossible to feel gloomy.

I even sang to myself as I pedaled along, swinging around the worst of the ruts and stones. I suppose I simply did not expect any other traffic on that quiet road; certainly I wasn't taking much care.

I shot around a corner a few hundred yards from the inn and found myself practically wheel to wheel with another cyclist. I was going far too fast to stop, but I did manage to swing my front wheel around. I was dimly conscious of an unknown and very attractive face as we both went down in a heap on the hard road.

A new friend

It was some moments before I got my breath, and as I struggled to sit up, a very soft, lilting voice gasped in my ear:

"Oh, I do hope you're not hurt!"

"I hope you're not, either," I retorted, trying to lift my bicycle off my legs. "It was all my fault. I was singing and not thinking—I just didn't expect——"

"Neither did I," said the other girl, and she helped me to slide my bicycle aside. Her own had somehow landed a couple of yards away. We scrambled to our feet and surveyed each other half shyly.

"Not much damage done," said the stranger, straightening her skirt and brushing her pretty green cardigan. Undoubtedly she was Welsh, but she had only the faintest of accents. She had a lively yet thoughtful face, very short, curly dark-brown hair, and really lovely features. Her eyes were brown and still held a rather concerned expression. "At least, I hope not. Your stockings——"

"An old pair," I said lightly, discovering a scratch on my hand. "We do seem to have been lucky. It was quite a smash. Aunt Mair's bike doesn't seem to have suffered much, either."

"You must be Catrin Drury," she said, picking up her own machine and examining it. It was almost a new one, and I was relieved to see that it, too, seemed undamaged. "I was coming to see you. I thought you might be lonely. I'm Gwenfron Williams from Gwyncefn Farm." And she waved her hand in the direction of the opposite hillside.

"It's awfully nice of you," I said, touched. "I *am* lonely. But how did you know about me?"

"I met Idris Jones last night," she explained. "Mr. Jones from the Collwyn Arms. He told me what had happened. A terrible thing, indeed! Poor Mrs. Davies! Have you heard how she is this morning?"

"I'm just on my way to telephone," I told her. "And to see Mr. Jones. I think I shall need some advice about the Priory."

Her brown eyes opened very wide.

"Are you going to stay?"

"I don't seem to have much choice," I said ruefully. And I told her about my chance visit to Aunt Mair, the accident, and the promise I had made at the hospital. She listened attentively and I thought, looking at her face, how very different she was from Olwen Jones. In those first few minutes I knew that I should like Gwenfron Williams.

"But that's very hard on you! Mrs. Davies didn't mind being alone there, but if you come from London and aren't used to the country——"

"I hated it last night," I said frankly. "But I'm determined to get used to it, and Dai's come home now. It won't be so bad with a dog."

"All the same, I don't think your aunt should expect——"

"She was ill and in pain. She didn't know what she was asking. And perhaps in a week or two she can make some other arrangement. She mentioned a friend at Llanrwst——"

We were pushing our bicycles slowly toward the inn, and Gwenfron looked very thoughtful.

"Oh, I think I know. An elderly lady who sometimes stays with her. But I shouldn't think she'd want—— Well, one never knows."

"I'll stick it out for the time being, anyway," I said. "I've explored now. Last night I didn't know what was hidden."

"You should have gone to the inn," she said.

"Perhaps. But it was partly that I'd promised, and partly that pride wouldn't let me. Olwen Jones——"

She grinned.

"Didn't you like our Olwen?"

I grinned back, feeling that we understood each other perfectly.

"We-ell, she so obviously expected me to quit."

"She knew you were from town. It's wrong of us, but we country folk never seem to expect much of towns-people."

"Don't you?" I stared at her, quite struck by the opposite point of view.

"No. They never seem to know how to cope with the

country. Not surprising, really, I suppose, and I know I should be very stupid on the London Tube, or trying to find the right bus."

"Oh, but the Tube's easy and so are the buses," I said quickly, and we both laughed. I went on: "I wouldn't ever have confessed it to Olwen, but I'm utterly out of my depth in the country. I was terrified of the valley last night. I'd honestly hate to live here, but I can learn to put up with it, I suppose, for a week or two. Isn't it frightful in the winter?"

Gwenfron shrugged.

"Well, it never seems so bad as Wrexham or Chester. I don't like wet pavements, and splashy cars, and people butting their way along with umbrellas. The country is always beautiful, even when it's muddy and cold, and you should see Nant Gwyncefn under snow."

"I never shall," I said with a slight shudder, and we laughed again, neither in the least put out by the other's point of view. I remembered the dark young farmer who had been so sardonically amused by my remarks and was grateful to Gwenfron. "Have you always lived here?"

"Yes," Gwenfron said. "But I went to school in Chester, living with an aunt during the week and only coming home at week ends. I love the farm. It's very old, you know. It's been here nearly as long as the Priory, so it's said. And there have been Williamses there for more than three hundred years. Actually, we own a good part of the valley." She said it very casually.

"Fancy its being as old as the Priory!" I marveled.

"Oh, that's only a story, though there are traces of a

much older building. The present house dates from 1605. There's a date stone."

We had reached the village by then and it was wrapped in Sunday peace. Though, when I came to think about it, it had been nearly as peaceful on Saturday afternoon. Smells of roasting meat came from the stone cottages, but there were few people in sight.

Gwenfron leaned her bicycle outside the post office.

"If you don't mind, I'll wait and hear the news about your aunt."

I went into the telephone kiosk and was soon through to the hospital. They were rather guarded. Aunt Mair had had a fair night, but was still very poorly.

"So that's that!" I said as I emerged again. "I shall have to try and get over to see her tomorrow. I said I'd take her some clean nightgowns and so on. She went with almost nothing, it was such an emergency. Oh, dear! I never, never thought that my Welsh holiday would turn into this!"

Gwenfron's brown eyes were very sympathetic.

"I think you're being very sporting about it. *And* courageous."

"I'm not," I said restlessly. "I hate it, really. I wanted to see lots more of Wales, and now it looks as though I'm going to be a prisoner here."

"You might learn more about Wales living for a time in one valley than you would if you wandered over several counties," she remarked, then laughed when she saw my disbelieving face. "Oh, well, come to supper tonight. That's really why I was on my way to look for you. About seven. I live with my mother and brother. Mother will be very pleased to see you. We don't get many strangers."

"Oh, I'd love to!" I cried, thankful to find a way of passing the evening. Though I knew that the dread of returning to the Priory would hang over me.

"Well, you cross that little bridge behind the inn, or else take the track that winds around beyond the Priory. There's another bridge there, but the road's rougher. Both tracks lead to the farm and then go on over the hills. I'll look for you and I'll love to have another talk." Then she nodded and rode away.

I made my way slowly to the inn and found that Mr. Jones was back from Chapel. The whole family was in the kitchen, where Mrs. Jones, looking hot and busy, was attending to their Sunday dinner. It smelled very appetizing.

Olwen, wearing a rather tight yellow jumper and slacks, was reading a magazine, and two boys of about ten and eleven were taking an air gun to pieces. I recognized them as the pair who had been playing by the river the previous afternoon.

"Well, indeed, and here's the girl herself!" cried Mr. Jones. "We were just talking about you, wondering how you fared last night."

"Very eerie it must be at the Priory in the dark!" said Mrs. Jones, hastily laying an extra place at the table. "Now you're here, girl, you'll be staying to dinner."

"Oh!" I said, feeling shy and rather awkward. "I didn't mean—— I just wanted to ask you about visitors to the Priory and so on."

"Well, you can be hearing about it over dinner; a nice

piece of Welsh lamb today. A long time it must be since you got a square meal in your stomach."

Well, it was, and I realized suddenly that I was ravenously hungry.

The two little boys were introduced as Inigo and Idwal, and they grinned at me uneasily, looking nearly as shy as I felt. The had rather sharp faces and inquisitive eyes, and I thought them very like Olwen.

It struck me suddenly that if I had not been there they would have been speaking Welsh, and the realization gave me a queer jolt. After all, Wales was a foreign country, and, in spite of my Welsh blood, I felt a stranger.

When we sat down to the meal I looked around curiously, wondering if I would have felt much farther from home in France or Italy. The inn seemed old, for there were thick black beams across the ceiling, and the fireplace had once been a great open inglenook. The cadence of the voices about me kept on striking me with renewed surprise and some pleasure. I liked the way that Mr. Jones and the little boys spoke English, but his wife and Olwen were much more shrill.

"You're nefer going to stay there at the Priory—a young town girl like you?" Mrs. Jones asked, serving me with a generous second helping.

"Yes, for the present," I said. "Someone has to look after the place and I promised Aunt Mair."

"You'll never stick it," Olwen remarked, and I noticed that she was careful not to say "nefer." It may sound unkind of me, but she seemed to be posing all the time, patting her hair and holding up her carefully polished nails.

Though, the previous night, she had seemed to despise me as someone from "town," she was in no sense a genuine country person. I knew that even then, and guessed that she tried to model herself on the characters in cheap magazines. There was a huge pile of them on the table at the window.

As her critical glance flickered over me, probably taking in all the faults in my appearance, I felt myself flushing.

"Oh, yes, I will," I said and wondered why it had been so easy to confess my fears and doubts to Gwenfron. Not for worlds would I have done the same to Olwen.

To change the conversation I asked her if she had a job, and she told me that she worked in a drugstore in Llangollen.

"Very good money," said her mother proudly. "And you'd nefer believe all the things she gets cheap."

Over the pudding Mr. Jones told me that I probably wouldn't get many visitors at the Priory so early in the year, except perhaps at week ends. There might, for instance, be a few that afternoon, as the day was so bright.

"Just you let them go round on their own, girl," he said cheerfully. "A shilling it iss and dear at the price. Just a lot of old stones."

"Aunt Mair told them about it," I said, and he waved his spoon at me.

"Well, nefer mind. In at one ear and out at the other it went, no doubt. Dead these hundreds of years, those old monks." Then, after a moment, he added: "The butcher calls Tuesdays and Fridays, and eggs and milk you can get from any of the farms."

"Collect them from here," said Mrs. Jones, who had disconcerted me throughout the meal by her curious, vaguely disapproving glances. "Indeed, I've no doubt it all seems very strange to you, and you from London."

"Yes," I agreed. "But I'll manage. I met a nice girl just now, and she asked me to supper tonight at Gwyncefn Farm."

Olwen positively jumped and said sharply:

"Gwenfron Williams? Well, indeed, so you're going to Gwyncefn?" She looked as though she thoroughly disliked the idea, and I wondered why.

But it was really time for me to be getting back to the Priory, and I said so, thanking them very much for the good meal.

"Very welcome you are," said Mr. Jones, and I thought that he, at least, was genuinely friendly.

The little boys disappeared outside, muttering together in Welsh, and soon afterward I took my leave. The sun was quite hot by then, and I walked slowly, pushing the bicycle, not really in any hurry to get back to the Priory. On my handlebars swung a can of milk given to me by Mrs. Jones.

"The cats will be pleased, anyway," I thought.

It seemed utterly incredible that twenty-four hours before, I had not set foot in Nant Gwyncefn, and yet in that short time I had made myself responsible for the Priory, got to know a whole Welsh family, and made friends with Gwenfron Williams. For I felt, with deep relief, that we would be friends. It was the one really bright spot in the whole business to know that there was an intelligent girl of my own age not too far away. Olwen simply didn't count; or, rather, if she did it was not in any friendly way.

As I went slowly under the spring green of the trees I told myself that it was silly to think that Olwen disliked me. It was probably just her manner. But for some reason she had simply hated the fact that I was going to supper at Gwyncefn Farm.

When the trees ended near the Priory I looked across the valley to where the farm stood on the opposite hillside, under the bracken-clad higher slopes. It appeared to be a big place, built of gray stone, with two gables and what seemed to be mullioned windows, though I could not be sure at that distance. It looked more like a manor house than a farm, and yet there were barns and cowsheds at a little distance, built of the same material.

Then I went on to the Priory and found Dai stretched out by the gate. He stood up when I approached and growled, and I spoke to him softly, for I did very much want to win his confidence.

Blackie was playing with a feather on the short grass of the cloister garth and he, at least, had no objection to having his tummy tickled.

When I straightened myself again I looked all around with a renewal of my doubt and incredulity. So big, so silent, so soaked in the atmosphere of centuries! The whole place looked beautiful in the sun, but sunlight didn't last forever.

I fetched three old saucers and arranged them on the garth, and before the milk was poured out, the three coal-black cats were sitting in a hopeful row. I caught Dai's eye and fetched an old dish, since he had told me so clearly that he liked milk, too. But he wouldn't wag his tail, or even approach the dish, until I had gone indoors.

I tidied up the house a little, then took my writing things and settled myself on a cushion against part of the cloister wall. And sitting there, with my back to the warm stones, I wrote another letter to Millicent, for it had occurred to me that I could do with more clothes. I had only the barest necessities with me, and if I was going to be asked out to meals—not to mention keeping up my morale in front of Olwen!—I should need some other things. I ended with a description of the Priory and told of my meeting with Gwenfron Williams, but I still made no mention of Aunt Mair's accident. Millicent would not get the letter till Tuesday, since it would only catch Monday's post, but with a bit of luck a parcel might reach me on Wednesday. My stepmother never wasted time.

"Wednesday!" I said aloud. "I shall still be here then." But I could scarcely believe it.

I was just addressing the envelope when there was the sound of a car on the road, and my heart leaped with alarm when it stopped outside the Priory gateway. A man and woman got out and approached me, smiling.

"Good afternoon. May we see the Priory, please?"

"Of course," I said, trying to sound as though I had been in charge of the ruins for years. "It's a shilling each, and there's a descriptive booklet that costs ninepence."

I ran indoors to get the tickets and one of the guidebooks, and when I returned they were standing in the nave of the church, discussing Norman, Transitional, and Early English architecture in a very knowledgeable way.

"It's such a beautiful setting," said the woman. "But then monks always seemed to build in the most idyllic places, especially the Cistercians. Let me see, now, what Order was this?"

For a moment I looked at her blankly, then I recollected something I had read in the guide that morning and also something that Aunt Mair had said.

"They were Augustinian Priors," I said with a faint gasp that I hoped was not noticeable. "Gwyncefn is built to exactly the same plan as Llanthony in Monmouthshire. And the Prior's house is used as a dwelling there, too."

After that I left them to it, and they seemed perfectly happy. They had clear voices, and the air was very still. Back on my cushion I caught occasional snatches of conversation as they wandered from the nave to the choir, and then into one of the transepts, the sacristy, and the chapter house. I heard them arguing about the position of the dormitory and the night stair to the church and felt horribly conscious of my own ignorance. A poor custodian, indeed! I would just have to learn more about the monastic way of life and what the various buildings had been used for.

They departed after half an hour or so, on their way to Valle Crucis Abbey only a few miles distant, and no one else came to disturb my peace. I definitely found the silence oppressive, and I longed for the sound of traffic and the sight of people going about their lives.

I was glad when it was time to go to Gwyncefn Farm. As I carried hot water up to my tower room the brightness of the day was already fading and the stone stairs were very cold. I suddenly felt lonely and desolate and I dreaded the night. I thought that I would never, never come to terms with the Priory ruins or with the country.

The dark young farmer

I washed, then brushed my hair till it shone. I put on my second skirt, a blue one, a paler blue blouse, and my scarlet jacket. Then I took up my handbag, made sure that I had the flashlight and that there were some well-placed candles and boxes of matches, and remembered at the last minute that Dai was probably hungry. I gave him some dog biscuits that I had found in the kitchen and some scraps of meat and shut him firmly into the house so that he would be there when I returned.

The double gates locked from outside with a heavy padlock, and that also gave me some relief. Then I set off to walk to Gwyncefn Farm. I was still rather early and, in any case, if I took the bicycle I would only have to push it up the hill to the farm.

The house looked even bigger than I had thought, as I approached by way of the road from near the village. The other two or three farms in sight were small and rather ugly, but against the hillside Gwyncefn Farm had a certain rather stern beauty. Somehow, I thought confusedly, in keeping with the Priory.

The lane wound a little, and here and there the hedges were quite high, shutting out some of the view. They also hid until the last moment the three black and white cows that blocked my way. Rounding the corner, I stared at them in horror, for to my own eyes they looked very big and fierce. They stared back at me without moving, and I remembered with greatly increased alarm that I was wearing red. Was it only bulls that minded red? I didn't know, and, in any case, the third animal might well be a bull. I couldn't see it properly, but it seemed to have very menacing horns.

My knees seemed to have turned to jelly, and I looked around wildly. On either side the hawthorn hedges were thick, but a few yards behind there was a gate if I could only reach it—but first I must take off my brilliant jacket.

The zipper stuck and refused to run smoothly downward, and one of the cows was moving toward me. No time to reach the gate! I saw that there was, after all, a slight gap in the hedge and plunged frantically toward it.

I was up the low bank in a moment and trying to push my way through the hawthorn. But it seized my skirt and even my hair, and I saw out of the tail of my eye that all three animals were advancing.

Then, with a stab of infinite relief, I heard a car approaching. The cows had gone on past, almost running, but I was still held fast in the gap.

The car stopped beside me and a voice said:

"Well, indeed!"

"It was the cows!" I cried. "I was right in their path. And my red coat——" Only then did I manage to release myself and turn around, in time to see my dark young farmer stepping out of the driver's seat. I recogized him immediately, though he was no longer in country clothes. Worst of all, I recognized that he was finding the situation an exceedingly amusing one, and I felt the hot color staining my cheeks, so that I'm sure they were as red as my jacket.

"So you're afraid of cows?" he said very quietly, but the amusement was still there in his dark eyes. "They shouldn't be on the road, and I'll have to try and get them through that gate. I suppose you couldn't pull yourself together enough to help? I assure you that they're really quite harmless."

I had had a bad fright, and I had nursed a feeling of dislike for him since that first meeting on the opposite hill. My knees were still weak, and I was suddenly filled with a feeling of absolute hatred for the country and for him. How dare he laugh at me, however silly I must have looked, tangled up in the hawthorn?

"I think you're rude and horrible!" I gasped. "You may not think much of townspeople, but at least they have better manners than country ones!" Then I managed to pass him and made rapidly for the next corner, not stopping until I reached a higher gate.

There I stopped and leaned against the bars, panting and still angry. I could hear him calling the cows and then the creak of the lower gate as it opened. After a few moments the three black and white animals moved rather skittishly into the field, and a minute or two later the engine started again and the car went slowly on toward the bridge and the village.

Only then did I fully realize what a complete fool I had made of myself. Not only had I looked like an idiot, but I had been abominably rude as well. I had talked about the bad manners of country folk, but I had not displayed very excellent ones myself.

The knowledge did nothing to calm my acute dislike of that dark Welshman. He had been in the wrong in the first place in looking so amused. He might at least have hidden his feelings and realized that not everyone had grown up among mud and muck and hulking great animals.

As I tidied my hair and dabbed powder on my decidedly shiny nose I tried to shut out the memory of his face, but it was still sharply with me as I began to climb the lane again. I could see his high cheekbones, his rather long mouth, his good teeth, and the one or two rather deep lines that furrowed his broad brow. He must be young— he didn't look more than twenty-three or twenty-four— and yet his face had an unusual look of maturity.

"Oh, stop it!" I said to myself. "No one mature would laugh like that. Forget the wretched man!"

Suddenly I was engulfed in a feeling of the most complete desolation I had ever known, and the reason was the very simple one that I didn't like being a stranger in a strange land and that I was lonely for my own kind; for the cheerful, uncomplicated youths who had shared my classes at the commercial college, and most of all for Penelope and our happy friendship.

But then I saw Gwenfron standing by a white gate, waving in a very welcoming way, and I went on more happily and confidently, for, though she was far from being Penelope, she attracted me very much.

Gwenfron led me into the lower part of the garden, which fell in terraces from the front of the house. It was vivid with aubrietia, which grew in purple waterfalls over the old gray stones and even in the crannies of the paths and steps, so that one could hardly avoid treading on it. There were wallflowers, too, filling the cool evening air with their fragrance, and I breathed deeply.

Gwenfron leaned on a wall and gazed down into the valley.

"Such a lovely evening! Doesn't the village look small and remote from here? The tiny chapel and the tiny school——"

"I shouldn't have thought there were enough children to fill even a tiny school," I said, leaning beside her and conscious that some of the peace of the scene was seeping into my uneasy and troubled mind. In the field just below us the lambs suddenly started up a shrill bleating, and a pair with black faces and black knees stood staring up at us as though they found us frightening but interesting.

"Oh, yes," Gwenfron said. "There are about twenty under eleven—the two Jones boys, and the three from the post office, and the rest from farms and cottages nearby. The older ones go to Llangollen in the school bus, and probably our own school *will* be closed one day. But it will be a great pity. They ought to stay in the valley when they're little."

"You love it all, don't you?" I asked curiously, glancing sideways at her face, so attractively framed in dark curly hair.

Gwenfron didn't answer for a moment, then she said slowly:

"I know you can't understand at all, but yes, I do. I was born here and I know everyone. I know every field and path and rock, every stone in the river. I can't bear it to change, but it does change all the time, of course. People get television and it alters their ideas. They want things different and I s'pose you can't blame them, but—— Oh, well, indeed, it's very silly of me!" She almost said "fery," but not quite.

I looked behind us at the house, which bore a television aerial.

"You have it, too. I shouldn't have thought—among the mountains——"

"Oh, we don't get bad reception, but I'm not keen about it, except for important events. It's nice to think you can sit in your own valley and see things happening in London. Important processions, and so on. Mother is so very fond of it, and Ifor likes it when he's tired."

"Ivor?" It was only later that I realized the name was spelled with the Welsh "f."

"My brother," she explained as we began to walk toward the house. "I've four more brothers, but they're all farming in Canada. They were like so many people— they grew restless here in Wales. Ifor's the next to the youngest boy, but Father left him the whole place. He never wanted the others to go away. But they're all doing very well—very well indeed. And Ifor never wanted to go away. He passed you on the road, I suppose, but you wouldn't know——"

I stared at her blankly, absolutely appalled.

"Was that—your brother? In the black Ford?"

Gwenfron looked rather astonished at my tone.

"Yes. He told me he thought he had met you on the hills yesterday. He was very sorry not to be at home to-night, but he's visiting friends in town. He often goes on Sundays. What's the matter, Catrin?"

"Nothing," I said. "I was just surprised." But dismay had me in a hard grip. I liked Gwenfron so much, and she was my only hope of congenial companionship in the valley. I liked the look of the house, too, and had hoped that I might be asked there often. And now fate had made me rude to Ifor Williams. Worse, it had made me take a hearty dislike to him, and I certainly didn't want to see *him* more than necessary.

He wasn't in the least like his sister. Gwenfron seemed so warm and friendly, and Ifor—I burned at the thought of our second unfortunate encounter and the fool I had looked, stuck on that bank like a ram in a thicket.

Gwenfron had bent to pick up a ginger kitten and was saying:

"Ifor works so hard. Help is very hard to get here."

"Do you—help?" I asked, for she didn't look at all as though she did farm work.

Gwenfron laughed at my tone.

"Oh, yes. I always have. I often milk, for one thing. It's mostly sheep, of course, but we keep a herd of Friesians, and some pedigreed pigs. Hens and ducks, too. The hens are my department when I'm home. And then there are things like haymaking. Lucky it is that I'm so handy!" And she gave me an amused grin. "If you stay long enough, Catrin, I'll teach you to milk."

"No, thank you!" I cried. "You might as well know— I'm afraid of cows. I met some on the road, and—— Well, they terrify me. They're so big and fierce-looking. I suppose you think that's very funny?" For the life of me I couldn't keep some bitterness out of my voice, and Gwenfron looked rather surprised.

"Oh, no. Lots of townspeople are afraid of cows. My aunt from Chester is scared stiff. Ifor teases her, but I know how she feels. Still, you've got lots of courage, or you wouldn't tackle the Priory. I thought that cows would be child's play after that."

I glanced back across the valley to where the great church stood up in the fields.

"I don't think I *have* tackled it. And if I never had to see it again I should be delighted. As soon as I can I'll go straight back to London, I think, without trying to see any more of Wales. I'm going to share an apartment with a friend and get a job in an office. Don't *you* ever feel—— Aren't you going to get a job?"

We were walking around the house by then, and Gwenfron stopped, with her chin on the kitten's soft head.

"I've been teasing you, really, Catrin. I *do* love it. I always miss it when I go away. But I'm restless, too. I'm going to have the summer at home—I only left school at Easter—and then I'm going to be a nurse."

"Oh!" I cried, very much taken aback. She seemed a surprising person. "But why? I was never in a hospital until yesterday. I don't think I'd like that any better than farming."

"I don't quite know," she said gravely, "but I've always meant to do it. It seems a good sort of life, and I like people. You'd have to, or it wouldn't work. I'm starting my training at Chester General on September first."

Then we went into the house through a side door and almost at once were met by a tall, brown-haired woman. She was very like Gwenfron, but I knew immediately that she was much more brisk and self-assertive. She held my hand firmly and said:

"So this is Catrin? My dear, I was so sorry to hear about poor Mrs. Davies's accident, and it's really very brave of you to stay alone at the Priory. Are you sure you're all right there?"

"Oh, yes, thank you," I said, feeling suddenly shy and extremely young.

"And you're really Mrs. Davies's niece? I don't think anyone knew she had any relatives."

"My mother was her youngest sister," I explained. "They lived near Llanberis—the family, I mean. My father met my mother when she was on a climbing holiday. She's dead. She died some years ago, and I've never seen Wales before."

"And she feels like an utter stranger," Gwenfron said in her sympathetic voice.

We went into a beautifully proportioned room with mullioned windows that looked across the valley. We were to eat at a polished table in the center window, and an old woman brought in soup almost immediately.

The meal was delicious and well served, and there was

a slightly shabby elegance about the whole place that surprised me. It didn't feel in the least like my idea of a farm.

As I ate, my eyes took in more details of the room, noting the stone fireplace with a carving that looked like a coat of arms, the dark oak paneling, the Welsh harp in a corner, and the beautifully arranged flowers. Everything looked very well cared for, though the carpet was old and faded, and the curtains and cushions were faded, too, to a soft, dim rose.

I felt more and more as though I were in a dream. So much had happened in so short a time. It even felt like days since that very different meal at the inn, and the events in the lane were fading a little, though I knew that it would be a long time before I could remember them calmly. At eighteen, especially when one is not very confident, almost the worst thing that can happen is to look silly in front of a superior person, and I hoped devoutly that Ifor Williams would stay with his friends in Llangollen until my visit was over.

The talk was mostly about the affairs of the valley, and I was surprised that it had a certain life of its own. For one thing, there was the Gwyncefn choir, which seemed to include nearly everyone.

"Very fine voices we have in Wales!" said Gwenfron, a trifle mischievously. "And even if a voice is not so fine it's soon drawn into the choir."

"It's a very good choir," said Mrs. Williams in her brisk way. "Otherwise it wouldn't have done so well last year at both the International Eisteddfod and the Welsh National Eisteddfod. Have you heard about the International Eisteddfod held in Llangollen each July, Catrin? It's a most wonderful thing. Quite an institution now."

I nodded.

"Oh, yes. And seen it on television. I think the folk dancing and singing must be wonderful."

"That's one of the most exciting things," Gwenfron said eagerly. "I love to be in Llangollen when the town's full of people from so many different countries, and all in their national costumes, too. All the different flags fly on the bridge, and of course there's the Red Dragon of Wales, and you rub shoulders with Americans and Italians and Spaniards, and even people from the Far East. One year we had a team from Bali; it was rather strange. Oh, it really is wonderful! You ought to try and come back for it, Catrin. Actually it's not just the town. Villages for miles around help to look after the people in the visiting teams and choirs. Last year we had Swiss people. An old man used to blow his alphorn out in the garden at dusk. It was a most heavenly sound, echoing back from the hills. And they yodeled in the moonlight, so that you could hear it all over the valley. Ifor and I went up on the hills to listen. It isn't only in that vast marquee that people sing and dance. Why, you should see——"

"And your aunt had some members of a German choir at the Priory. They practiced in the nave," said Mrs. Williams.

"Oh!" I cried. "But could she—— Can she speak German?"

"No, I don't think so. But no one worries about a little thing like that, and probably some of them could speak some English. One village took in a whole Spanish dancing team, and none of them could exchange a word all week. But they all had a wonderful time and parted the best of friends."

It certainly sounded most exciting and impressive, and my ideas changed a little more. I had thought of the town of Llangollen, and the villages nearby, as being so remote and cut off. I had quite forgotten that, for a few summer days each year, it was one of the centers of the world. The thought of a German choir singing in the nave of the ruined church astonished me, and curiosity began to stir.

"Perhaps I might try and come," I said cautiously. "But I expect I shall have a job by then." July seemed a long way away.

"Gwenfron played the harp last year. She's won a great many prizes."

We had finished the meal by then and were sitting around the fire drinking coffee. My eyes immediately went to the shining instrument, and once again Gwenfron presented a new aspect.

"Oh, I would so love to hear it played. My mother used to play the harp when she was young, so she once told me. They had a harp at the farm, by the old Welsh dresser in the kitchen. I'd forgotten until now."

Gwenfron rose slowly, and I realized how graceful she was. More than ever I wanted to know her better, so that I could understand what it was that made her enjoy so many things—milking cows, looking after hens and ducks, playing the Welsh harp, and feeling that to be a nurse was the right life for her.

It was still quite light outside, but the room was growing shadowy. And through the shadows rippled the notes of that lovely instrument. Somehow they clutched at my heart, so that loneliness and pride and pain fell away and I was strangely, warmly happy, as though I had known that house, that room, for years.

At first it was music that I had never heard before . . . sometimes little more than clear chords and soft cascades of sound, but suddenly Gwenfron began to sing "All Through the Night" in Welsh. Her voice was lovely, and the song, the language, sent me straight back to my childhood. How often had Mother sung me to sleep with that very air? It had always seemed part of my life; it and the one that followed—"David of the White Rock."

It was only when, at last, the music died away and Gwenfron came back to the fire that I remembered the darkening valley, the Priory, and all my problems.

"Thank you very much," I said with a little difficulty. I had been more moved than I would ever have been able to admit. "It was beautiful. I hope you'll play and sing to me again?"

"You like music?" Gwenfron asked.

"Yes. My mother was very musical. She had a lovely voice, and she took me to concerts when I was little. But I think I ought to go now. I—I'd rather be back before it grows dark."

"It won't be dark for some time," said Mrs. Williams. "But it always grows very shadowy in the valley, especially at the far end. I wanted to talk about London, but perhaps next time. You'll come again, of course, my dear?"

"Oh, yes, please. I should like to," I said as I rose.

Gwenfron fetched her coat and my jacket.

"I'll walk down to the Priory with you."

"Oh, but—— It *will* be getting really dark by the time you get back."

Gwenfron laughed.

"I don't mind the dark. I always have a flashlight in my pocket, but I rarely use it. We don't need street lamps. In fact, we'd hate them."

"I think a nice row of them would be splendid!" I said, and we all laughed.

Outside the air was cold, but smelled very sweet. Gwenfron walked so fast, and had such a long stride, that I had quite a job to keep up with her. We went by the other track to the bridge over the river, close under the crags. The water came tumbling down in a series of little falls, and to my mind it was very eerie there.

When we approached the Priory I couldn't help jumping nervously as an owl hooted somewhere in the ruins.

Gwenfron put her hand on my arm.

"I can see you don't like it, but owls don't do any harm at all. I always think they're rather nice. I'll just wait while you lock yourself in. Where's Dai?"

"In the house," I told her thankfully.

"Then you'll be all right. He's an alert creature."

"Oh, of course," I said, trying to sound casual, "I'll be perfectly all right. And thank you for such a lovely evening."

Gwenfron nodded and then said good night as I closed and locked the gates. I heard her tramping away over the stony track, singing to herself.

I ran across the cloister garth and thrust home the huge old key. With the door locked behind me I felt more or less safe, and it was certainly a relief to have Dai there, even though he gave me no sort of welcome, but just sniffed suspiciously at my feet.

I poked up the kitchen fire and stood there staring into the flames. My mind was a teeming mass of new impressions, of thoughts and memories and the consciousness of my many problems. And worst of all was the knowledge that I didn't like Gwenfron's brother and that he, presumably, didn't like me.

I *wanted* to go back to Gwyncefn Farm; I wanted it as much as I wanted anything, so long as I was a prisoner in that valley. But it wasn't going to be easy. It was going to be very difficult.

A shock for Catrin

I had thought that I had laid some of the ghosts by exploring the house and the ruins, but in many ways my second night was much worse than my first one. For even before I went up to my tower the wind was rising and rain began to fall in sheets. In spite of the glowing fire and the light of several candles, I felt haunted by the thought of the black night outside and the fact that no one was nearer than the inn.

I looked at Dai and at the three black cats sitting cozily in front of the hearth, and was glad of their company, but it did not stop my feeling as though, somehow, I had been left alone in the world. As though there was nothing beyond the ruins but blackness; no people, no lights anywhere. In that mood I could not even imagine London going on as usual. It was only ten o'clock. People would just about be starting to come out of the theaters; the restaurants would be full; the buses would be traveling down Piccadilly and the Haymarket and Shaftesbury Avenue. I told myself all that, but it made no difference. I felt so frighteningly alone that I could have cried and perhaps never stopped.

"I've got to get away tomorrow!" I told myself. "I've got to tell Aunt Mair that I must get back to London, and they'll have to find someone to take her place until she's better. Yes, tomorrow I'll go and see her at the hospital, then I'll come back and get my things and go to a hotel in Llangollen for the night. The day after that I'll go home."

Why I didn't plan to take my few possessions with me to Wrexham I don't quite know. Perhaps it was the subconscious feeling that nothing could be arranged definitely until I had seen and spoken to Aunt Mair.

In the end I had to leave the warm kitchen and climb the tower by flashlight, clutching my hot-water bottle. I thought that if I had to spend one more night at the Priory I would sleep in Aunt Mair's bed and wondered why it had not occurred to me before.

There were no curtains at the big window in my room, and the rain was beating against the black, shiny glass. The wind seemed to shake the tower, and it was abominably eerie. Surely it wasn't altogether cowardly of me to be so afraid?

The kitten had followed me up the spiral stairs, and when I climbed into the big bed he settled himself close to me, purring contentedly. His presence, and the knowledge that Dai was loose in the house and would surely guard me well, were my only comforts. And yet I knew that I didn't need to be guarded from anything tangible.

It was the wind, the wild rain, and the atmosphere of the ancient building that caused my fear and tension. I had been a fool, a proud fool, to think that I could ever stay there. But I would forget my pride the next day.

I lay awake for hours, trying to lull myself to sleep with thoughts of Gwenfron's lovely harp playing, but the memory of Gwenfron only brought back, inevitably, the thought of her brother. Well, if I was leaving the next day I need never see Ifor Williams again, and he would soon forget the girl who was afraid of cows and who thought country people were half dead.

The wind increased in the middle of the night, and I marveled that there could be such a gale in that deep valley. But perhaps it was acting as a sort of funnel, and the limestone cliff was throwing the gusts back at the Priory ruins. Yet they must have stood nine hundred years of weather . . . the monks themselves must have lain awake and listened to the wind and the rain.

That thought made me wonder what they had been like, those men who had built and lived in the Priory. Their sleeping quarters had gone, but they must have been of stone like my own tower room. No feather beds, though, for men dedicated to the religious life . . .

On and on and on went my thoughts, and at last, about half past three, I slept.

I awoke at half past eight to a brilliantly sunny morning. The wind was still blowing, but the rain had gone; the whole scene was as bright as a railway poster. The hills above the high arches of the nave were green with uncurling bracken, there were great white puffs of clouds

in the dazzling blue, and some golden wallflowers growing high in the ruins looked almost unbelievably vivid.

Gone was fear and the worst of my loneliness, but I
was firm in my resolution. Tomorrow morning I would
awaken in a hotel bedroom and then I'd travel to Chester
and catch the first good train to London.

I spent the morning tidying up the house and seeing
that everything was in order. Also I packed a small suitcase with things that Aunt Mair might need and put the
ten pounds from the silver teapot in my handbag, ready
to hand over to her. She might easily need some money.

Nant Gwyncefn, Gwenfron had told me, was served by
a small, shabby bus run by a local man. Three times a
day it went into Llangollen, and three times returned to
the Gwyncefn post office. There was one soon after one
o'clock, so I had an early lunch, fed Dai and the cats, and
set off to the post office.

Already sitting in the bus was Mrs. Jones, gossiping in
Welsh with several other women. They all looked at me
rather avidly and Mrs. Jones said:

"Well, girl! And how are you today? And how's the
Priory? Not blown down in the gale?"

"No, not blown down," I said. "I'm going to see my
aunt."

"Well, now, seeing you with a suitcase, I thought you
were off! You'll be giving her our best wishes? Very sorry
about it we all are. If I'd known, you could have been
taking her some of my homemade jam and some eggs."

"I'll get her some fruit or something," I said, and then
the driver appeared, a small, dark man, who greeted
everyone familiarly in Welsh and looked me over curi-

ously. Soon afterward we were off, bumping and rattling over the stony road.

In the brilliant sun the valley looked beautiful. The river sparkled, the lambs capered in the fields, and the smell of hawthorn blew in through an open window. But I scarcely noticed. I was thinking about Aunt Mair and planning to have a good dinner at a hotel that night. No more Youth Hosteling for me! I had had more than enough of primitive conditions.

In a very short time we were speeding through Berwyn, where the swing bridge spanned the madly foaming Dee, and soon the town of Llangollen appeared ahead.

Mrs. Jones turned around and shouted to me over the din made by the old vehicle:

"And how are you liking it in Wales? You'll not be staying long, I'm sure. Want to get back to your gay life in London town."

For some totally mysterious reason, that put my back up slightly. I had been dreaming of comfort and of what I would do when I got back. A theater, a new film, perhaps a dance with Penelope and some of our friends. I had made up my mind to go, and there was really no reason why I should not tell Mrs. Jones so at once. But something about her tone and the look in her sharp dark eyes made me say:

"I don't have such a gay life in London—only sometimes. When I get back I shall have to work."

"Olwen wass saying only last night, she said, 'Mam, two or three days I give her and no more. Even with supper at Gwyncefn Farm stands to reason she won't stick it.' "

"Olwen seems to know a lot about me," I said rather coldly, and she laughed.

"Fery shrewd iss our Olwen. And wass *he* there last night?"

"Who?" I asked blankly, being taken up with wondering what they would all say when I had gone.

"Why, Ifor Williams."

"Oh!" I said, and annoyed myself by blushing. "No. He was visiting friends. But I don't see——"

She nodded, as though with satisfaction.

"Olwen thought she saw the Ford going toward the town. Fery sharp eyes our Olwen hass. So you've not seen him?"

"Yes, I've seen him," I said, wondering why it was of so much interest to her. Then the bus stopped and I seized the case with Aunt Mair's things in it and hurried away toward the Wrexham bus.

In Wrexham I bought Aunt Mair some oranges and grapes and a box of cookies, and, decidedly laden, presented myself at the hospital.

"Visiting at night," said the little Welsh porter, shaking his head at me.

"But I telephoned yesterday and was told that I could see my aunt for a short while this afternoon. I can't get here at night," I cried, suddenly rather frantic.

He let me through and I made my way to the ward. A Sister met me near the entrance.

"Mrs. Davies? Oh, you're her niece, my dear? And you've brought her things? Good!"

"How is she?" I asked, and she said quietly:

"Not too well, I'm afraid. Her leg has given her a lot

of pain, and there was a good deal of shock. She's sleeping now, I think, but I'll make sure." She sent a nurse to see, and the pretty girl came back quickly. I thought of Gwenfron and tried to imagine her in uniform, looking after sick people.

"She's awake, Sister. But she seems very queer. I——"

The Sister frowned at her, shaking her head a little.

"Well, five minutes, my dear. Just sit by her and say a few words. Nothing to worry her."

"But I *must* talk to her!" I said frantically. "Honestly I must." And then I found myself pouring out the whole tale. She listened sympathetically, which was nice of her, as I'm sure she was very busy.

"I see. It's quite a problem, and I'm sorry. Perhaps in a few days—— But I'm afraid she's here for a long time. Her blood pressure is abnormally high, about as high as it can possibly be. If she hadn't had this accident, something would have happened soon. It's going to be a long business—that and her leg."

"How long?" I begged with a sinking heart, for I had been buoyed up by the knowledge that people *did* manage to get around, even with broken legs. I had thought that the limb would be put in a plaster cast and then——

"It's too early to say," she said. "Can't you make some other arrangement at this Priory? There must be someone."

"But I promised," I said wretchedly. "I can't break it without telling her."

"Well, I'm afraid you certainly mustn't tell her. Anything in the least upsetting might have very serious consequences."

So I sat beside Aunt Mair for exactly five minutes, just holding her hand and telling her that everything was quite all right. When I went away I was told that I could slip in any afternoon I could manage, and then I was out in the sunshine again, facing the knowledge that I was not free of the Priory. So it was just as well that I hadn't said anything to Mrs. Jones.

"It'll be a disappointment for Olwen, anyway," I thought. "Even if she is so very shrewd. A pity she doesn't take after her nice father. I like that little man!"

I had tea in a café and then traveled back to Llangollen. As luck would have it, Olwen was on the six-o'clock bus, and she immediately came to sit by me. She looked very smart, but Millicent would have had something caustic to say about her make-up. It was decidedly flamboyant, but it suited her rather hard good looks.

"And how is life with you, Catrin *fach?*"

I didn't care to be called "Catrin dear" by Olwen, but I smiled as pleasantly as I could and said that it might be worse, I supposed. London had retreated again, and I was faced with another night at the Priory, but once more pride won.

We made conversation all the way to Gwyncefn village, and it began to dawn on me that, though she certainly despised me for knowing so little about the country, Olwen's main feeling was one of jealousy because I was lucky enough to be a Londoner.

"London is lovely!" she said.

"Do you go often?"

She shrugged, just as the bus stopped outside the post office and we all lurched to our feet.

"Only once. When the play was first on. We went by coach and traveled back through the night. Very exciting it was!"

I hadn't the slightest idea what play she was talking about and hadn't a chance to ask because she went off toward the inn at such a rapid pace, in spite of her high heels.

Tired and dispirited, I followed, and she had gone indoors by the time I passed the inn. But Mr. Jones was in the garden, hoeing between his fine cabbage plants, and he greeted me cheerfully.

"And how iss your aunt? Good news, I hope!"

"No, it's rather bad," I told him. "She's very ill, and I couldn't even talk to her properly."

"So you're stopping at the Priory, girl?"

"Yes," I said briefly.

"Fery brave you are, and eferyone thinks so. Now, indeed, nefer be lonely. There'll always be a welcome here and fery friendly you'll find the people of the valley. Mrs. Roberts from Collwyn Farm"—he waved his hand along the valley—"wass saying only just now, 'Tell that poor girl to come and see us of an evening. Fery pleased we'll be, and we with the fine new TV set.' You needn't lack company, see."

I was moved by his kindness and by Mrs. Roberts's message. In the bus both going and returning I had thought the people alien and perhaps not very friendly, the way they had stared at me. But perhaps it was just that they shared a language that I scarcely knew, and that I was a "foreigner."

"It's very nice of you all," I said, and thought that I

might be heartily glad to visit people. The Robertses' fine new television set would be ten times better than lonely evenings in the ruins, with not even a radio for company. Aunt Mair's old set was one that worked on a battery, and I hadn't been able to get a sound out of it. Of course there was Gwyncefn Farm, but I couldn't expect to go there all that often. Gwenfron probably had lots of friends and plenty to occupy her.

But when I came in sight of the Priory gates, there was Gwenfron sitting on a stone, with her bicycle propped up beside her. She had a basket on her knee and waved cheerfully.

"Hi, Catrin!"

My heart immediately felt much lighter.

"Oh, now nice of you to come! I was dreading arriving back, and—and——"

"Mother thought that you mightn't have been able to do much shopping yet," Gwenfron remarked. "So I've things for supper here and a bottle of cider. I thought you'd like me to stay."

How different the Priory seemed with Gwenfron's company to keep my fear and problems at bay. She showed me how to deal with the lamps and the oil stove for cooking, and also helped me to move into Aunt Mair's room. Then we had a merry meal, with Dai so far unbending as to lean his head against Gwenfron's knee. Not *my* knee, unfortunately, but I was relieved to see him looking happier.

At first, in spite of my pleasure in her company, I was a little shy and on the defensive, for I wondered if Ifor had told her about my behavior in the lane. I didn't know which I would have minded most: that he had made me out to be gauche and rude or a silly little coward.

But Gwenfron never mentioned her brother, and I began to hope that he had said nothing. Not that Gwenfron would have blamed me for being afraid of cows, but I had small doubt that, if he had wanted to, Ifor Williams could have made a good story of our second meeting.

After the meal we had coffee and sat by the fire to drink it, and Gwenfron asked me to tell her about my life in London. So I told her all about the commercial college, and Penelope and our plans, and how we would have such fun together. Money might be tight at first, but we would manage to go to films and plays occasionally. Penelope liked French and Italian films, and we were both keen on the theater.

Gwenfron listened with attention.

"I love the theater, too, but I don't get many chances. Sometimes Ifor and I go to Liverpool for a matinee. There are often pre-London shows there and ballet companies."

"I used to get teased a bit at school for being a highbrow," I said. "But I'd rather see intelligent plays and read intelligent books. Most of the girls never did more than go to an American musical, and they read the most frightful tripe. Penelope's older than I, and she's got brains. She'd have gone to the University, but her father died and she had to earn her living quickly."

"I wonder if you saw *Death of the Dragon?*" Gwenfron asked. "It ran at the Royal Crown Theater for six weeks and got a lot of notice, but it was never transferred to another theater."

I looked at her eagerly.

"The Welsh play? Oh, yes, I saw it twice. I thought it was one of the most wonderful plays I'd ever seen." I jumped up and crossed to the shelves in a corner where Aunt Mair kept some of her books and seized a slim volume. "Afterwards, when it was published, I bought a copy and I brought it with me to Wales." I stood there looking down at the lettering on the cover: *Death of the Dragon,* a play in three acts, by Ifor Caradoc.

"We all went up for the first night," she said, almost dreamily. "It was wonderful! Oh, indeed, I shall never forget! It was a marvelous cast, wasn't it? Half the people in the valley went, and Ifor had to go on stage. I think Mother could have burst with pride, though she never said much."

It was like a blow in the face. For several moments I simply hadn't words. Then I choked out:

"Ifor? What do you mean?"

"He wrote it," she said. "I suppose you couldn't know. His name's Ifor Caradoc Williams, but he left off the Williams because of Emlyn. He said there was only one playwright with that name. Oh, Ifor's very clever; very clever indeed. He's a bard, too. At the Welsh National Eisteddfod——"

But I didn't hear what she was saying about the Eisteddfod. I was back in the Royal Crown Theater, seeing that sharp, bitter, and moving play about the fight of a bleak Welsh village against a great English city. There was a plan to flood the valley to provide water for the city, and the village would be lost. I heard again the Welsh voices and remembered the wonderful characterizations.

The old schoolteacher, who had given his life to each generation of village children; the innkeeper's wife, whose only child was buried in the little churchyard; the two young people who planned to marry and carry on an ancient farm. I remembered the teacher standing in the village street, looking at the little houses and then up at the slaty hills. I heard his voice, for I knew some of the speeches by heart:

"And it will all be forgotten. The water will lie over the smokeless chimneys and over the little gardens, washing in through the windows of these houses where people have been born and lived and died. Nothing will stop it—— Oh, indeed, nothing at all! Sometimes the water will be blue with the reflection of the sky and sometimes wind-tossed, and under it will lie all we remember. Old it is, that school building, but good for another generation yet. The red dragon of Wales is old, too, and will not be able to fight this thing that has come to us."

But some had fought for that grim little village in the wild hills, the oldest and the youngest, and some of their speeches had been sheer poetry.

Death of the Dragon had brought me to Wales. It was while seeing it that I had known that I must see my mother's country. And its author was the dark young farmer whom I had despised as an ignorant countryman! I could have died with shock.

Later Gwenfron told me that the Liverpool Repertory Company was going to put on *Death of the Dragon* soon and that Ifor would be going up once or twice for rehearsals. But I remember very little else about that evening.

It was nearly dark when Gwenfron went, but I was far too occupied with my thoughts to feel any fear or uneasiness that third night. I had imagined myself in a hotel, and then speeding back to London, but I didn't even remember to curse fate for forcing me still to be in Nant Gwyncefn.

I only know that, as I went to bed in Aunt Mair's room, I was just about the most humble girl in Britain. Never again would I leap to quick, standard conclusions—or I vowed to myself that I would not. Life evidently just wasn't like that. You couldn't say, "Countrymen are dull and half dead" or "Townspeople are always intelligent and alive." You met a man on the hills who looked exactly like your imaginary picture of any young farmer, and you didn't know that he had written a thought-provoking and highly respected play and that he was a bard. And he couldn't know—how on earth could he be expected to? —that you weren't really a silly little chit with ready-made ideas and a temper.

I slept, but I awoke in the middle of the night, wondering what I could possibly say to Ifor Williams when I met him again. If I could avoid him I would; it seemed the only way. He had laughed at me, and how right he had been, but I could never bring myself to tell him so. All the same, deep in my heart, I still resented that laughter. I resented it until I remembered all he had done; how much bitter and yet strangely magical awareness he had given me in a London theater.

I was a mass of conflicting feelings.

ℙrotecting the Priory

Nearly five more days passed and I was still at the Priory, with no definite news of Aunt Mair and the future still blank. Every time I went to the hospital I hoped to be able to have some real conversation with my aunt, but, though she was rather better, she was very weak and easily upset, and the Sister always hovered somewhere near. I expect she knew that I was desperately anxious, but I would never have said anything to upset Aunt Mair.

It was Saturday again, and as I pushed the old mower over the cloister garth and the short grass of the nave I looked back over those days with the incredulity that was rapidly becoming part of my mental attitude. Last Saturday I had left the Youth Hostel and eaten my picnic lunch high on the hills. I had seen the Priory after a hail shower, standing up in the shining fields, and had pulled that fatal bell rope, bringing my aunt to the door. If *only* I had turned away and gone on to the next hostel! If I had done that I should never have found myself guardian of Gwyncefn, and a very reluctant guardian, too.

It had been the longest week of my life, even longer than the first rather unhappy week I had spent at the commerical college. I didn't even feel the same girl as the one who had tramped down the lane, swinging her mackintosh. That girl hadn't known anything about being alone in an ancient Priory; nothing about a remote community; nothing about young farmers who brought Welsh problems sharply to life on a London stage.

Since that unfortunate Sunday meeting I had seen Ifor Williams twice, but only in the distance. Once I had been walking across the field path from the Priory and he was driving a scarlet tractor in a field across the river, and once I had caught a glimpse of him in the streets of Llangollen, striding along as though he were in a great hurry. I hadn't wanted him to see me, for I still didn't know what I was going to say when the moment was forced on me.

Twice he had been to Liverpool, and I think it was coincidence that Gwenfron asked me up to the farm those days. She showed me the poultry, the pedigreed pigs, and the barns, cowsheds, and stables, and, since the weather was bright and almost warm, I quite enjoyed myself, though I strenuously resisted her suggestion that she should teach me to milk.

"We don't have a machine, as it's such a small herd. Catrin, you'd do it well. You've got sensitive hands, I'm sure."

"I'm sensitive in other ways, too," I said quickly. "I *hate* the thought of being so near one of those great

beasts!" And I kept a wary eye on all gates while I was
at the farm. It was good training in gate shutting, at
least, to be afraid of freeing cows or those big, wicked-
looking pigs.

Millicent had sent my things, so I was able to wear
slacks and a jersey at the farm. Gwenfron wore breeches
and boots and looked very businesslike. I admired her
more and more for her varied gifts and knew that there
were depths in her that I had certainly not explored.
Perhaps I never should. Friendly and talkative on the
surface, she was in some ways strangely withdrawn, and
when she was thoughtful I thought once or twice that she
was very like her brother, after all. Her face seemed to
take on the same lines as his, and she looked older than
her years.

A week! And in that time Llangollen had grown quite
familiar. I knew which shops I liked to visit and had my
little pleasures. Morning coffee in a café, before catching
the eleven-thirty bus back with my shopping; standing in
one of the embrasures on the ancient stone bridge, looking down at the Dee foaming over the shining black rocks;
seeing the trains stopping at the station close to the river,
some of the coaches labeled to Dolgelly and Barmouth
and other places that once I would have liked to see. Now
the trains mostly meant to me an escape that I could not
take, and I watched enviously the lucky travelers who
were going the other way toward Chester.

On Friday, before going to the hospital, I climbed the
steep hillside to the ruins of Castell Dinas Bran and
looked all around in the clear light. The town far below,
the Berwyns, the harsh, rocky ridges of the Eglwysegs, the

green folds of the tumbling fields, and the higher mountains in the distance. . . . Yes, the wide view was lovely.
In the sunny weather I could not deny that, but I would
have bartered it gladly for a sight of Hampstead Heath
or Hyde Park.

In a week I had got to know quite a number of people:
Mrs. Parry, who kept the tiny post office and general
store, with her shrill pleasure in life and her three beautiful little girls. The youngest, at five, was only just starting
to learn English; so far she had only spoken in Welsh.
The Roberts family, whose only luxury was the television
set; the Griffiths from Llanbryn Farm; the shepherd, old
Rhys Morgan, who worked for Ifor Williams; Huw Jones
·—no relation to the Joneses at the inn—who also worked
at Gwyncefn Farm . . . gradually they were becoming
clear to me, distinctive personalities. And they had all
been kind, if rather avidly curious, about my continued
stay at the Priory.

In a week, too, I had learned to find the Priory ruins
more familiar, though they still seemed eerie to me in the
dark. I found the house more familiar, also, and was surprised that housework and cooking were not the burdens
I had always thought them. By Wednesday I had started
on some of the books in the crowded bookcases, supposing
that I'd better discover as much as I could about the
monastic way of life. My few visitors had seemed so horribly knowledgeable that I found it rather humiliating
not to know more. And it certainly held a fascination. I
found myself growing quite absorbed in a thick old book
that told the history of Gwyncefn Priory. It must have
been quite an adventure for those first monks, who chose

the site in the valley and built their great church and living quarters of the local stone.

I even went, on the second Sunday I was at Gwyncefn, to see the ruins of the Cistercian Abbey of Valle Crucis, a few miles away on the other side of the Dee; and how beautiful it looked as I crossed the big meadow in the May sunshine—the high rose window, the broken arches, against the green hills, and the buttercups beginning to open at my feet.

Valle Crucis, I found, had a restored chapter house and it had kept its dormitory. To my astonishment I found myself quite annoyed about that, though it was interesting to see where the monks had slept. If only more of Gwyncefn had been spared! And yet our church was far greater and in better repair than that at Valle Crucis.

I talked for a while to the man who took my money, and he seemed interested to hear that I was in charge of Gwyncefn Priory.

"You'll have to watch people," he said. "Some of them are terrible. Papers and cigarette packs flung down, and as for people who *will* carve their initials——"

"I haven't had many people yet," I said. "But I couldn't bear it if they did things like that. Why *should* they want to carve their initials? Surely they'd rather see a building beautiful and unspoiled? But most of the people who've come to Gwyncefn know more than I do myself."

"You wait and see!" he said darkly.

What with visiting Aunt Mair, shopping, cooking, and going to Gwyncefn Farm, I hadn't had much time to be really lonely, and the weather had turned so glorious that there were times when I decided that the country wasn't so bad, after all. I took to eating my meals, when possible, out on the cloister garth, and I was already getting quite sun-tanned. I felt different, and my face and limbs *looked* different. The healthy tan certainly suited me, and my hair was shining as it had never done before. I felt well and was hungry for every meal, and I told myself with satisfaction that, in spite of everything, my queer, enforced sojourn in the valley wasn't being so bad.

I even found that I enjoyed gardening, though I had never taken the slightest interest in Millicent's window boxes. There was a certain pleasure to be had from the smell of freshly cut grass and the sight of flower beds denuded of weeds.

I had still not confessed to my father and stepmother that I was alone at the Priory, and I hoped it would not be necessary until I returned. I was into my second week, and I had only promised to stay "for a week or two." On Sunday evening, when I was waiting for Gwenfron to arrive, I was tidying some papers and found a postcard with a view of Llanrwst. There was an address, though the card was only signed, "Yours, Maggie." Aunt Mair's friend!

Immediately I wrote her a note, explaining what had happened and begging her to come to the Priory if she could. I addressed it to "Miss Maggie——" and hoped that she would receive it. If only she were willing to come, my problems would be over.

On Monday morning I was just starting to cook my lunch—it was surprising how handy I was getting with the oil stove—when there was a sudden racket outside. A horn sounded, then car doors banged and there was the shrill sound of children's voices. Dai immediately began to bark wildly, and I shut him up in the kitchen and went to investigate. A large and very shabby shooting brake had been driven through the gates, almost onto the cloister garth, and a man and woman and three boys of about nine, eight, and six were all advancing across the grass. The boys were yelling and chasing one another, and certainly very effectively putting an end to the peace of centuries.

The man carried a large basket, and the woman a smaller one, out of which lemonade bottles protruded. It was a hot morning, at least within the sheltered precincts of the Priory, and the man wore an open-necked shirt.

"Good morning," I said. "Do you want to see the Priory? It's a shilling each for adults and half price for children."

The man fumbled for money with his free hand.

"We'd like a look around later, but first we're going to have a picnic, if it's all right with you, Miss."

"Oh, yes," I said as I handed him the tickets. "Do have your picnic lunch here."

"I suppose you couldn't manage a cup of tea?" the woman asked longingly. She looked rather a harassed creature, with a crumpled frock and untidy hair. "I broke the flask before coming out—lads will bother so—and I don't care for lemonade. Nasty gassy stuff!"

"Oh, I expect I could manage a pot of tea," I said, willingly enough. Aunt Mair would probably have done the same.

"Good!" the man said. He had put the basket down and was lighting a cigarette. The empty pack was flung on the garth, and I opened my mouth to protest, then thought I'd better wait. "Fine weather we're having! Makes it worth while to take an early holiday. And it's good for the kids. They've all had measles, and the doctor said to get them out."

"They seem full of energy," I remarked rather wryly, for the eldest was already trying to climb the remains of the nearest wall. "Please keep them off the stones. For one thing, it's dangerous, and for another, it will damage the building."

"Now, then, Harry! Do give over!" the woman cried, as though she had said it many times before. "Come over from Ellesmere Port, we have. It makes a nice change."

I waited until I saw that Harry had "given over," though he immediately started to chase poor dignified Bledig, and then I went into the house to make the tea and see that my lunch was not burning.

When I returned with the tray they were sitting in a row against the wall of the chapter house, and the boys were eating so heartily that they seemed safely occupied.

The kitchen window looked the other way, but peace seemed to reign while I ate my lunch. I had just got to the cheese stage when there was a most appalling din, and I hurried along the passage to the open front door.

The spot where the picnic had taken place looked frightful, with scattered paper bags, chocolate papers, and empty bottles. One bottle had been broken, and the pieces glinted in the sun. But it was not that that at first held my attention. The eldest boy was some way up the ruined tower, and the two younger ones were fighting fiercely, their stout shoes kicking up the smooth turf of the nave. Of the father there was no sign, but the woman was sitting on the base of a pillar, smoking a cigarette and making ineffectual pleas to the boys to "behave."

I was furious. I looked from the boys to the frightful litter and something came over me. I dashed across to the two fighters and grabbed each with a firm hand. Wrenching them apart, I gave each one a violent shake and said sharply:

"Behave yourselves at once! Look what you're doing to the grass! And a church, ruined or otherwise, is no place to fight in. And as for you"—coldly and clearly to the child on the tower—"come down this instant!"

I must have sounded very "schoolmistress-y," but I was shaking with anger, and certainly my tone had the desired effect. The two younger ones were silent, staring at me with their mouths comically open and their fists clenched, and Harry began to climb down. I had to resist the strong temptation to seize him as he came within reach and give him a hard smack on the bottom.

"I wasn't doing no harm," he said sullenly.

"Of course you were," I retorted, quite regardless of the fact that his father had appeared out of the north transept. "You might harm yourself seriously, in any case, but that's your lookout. I'm in charge of this Priory, and it hasn't stood for nine hundred years to be further ruined by ill-mannered little boys." Then I turned to the woman. "I'm very sorry, but I think you'd better go. But first please clear up that mess in the cloister, including every bit of broken glass. There is a waste-paper box not two yards away from where you were sitting, you know, and——"

"Here, Miss, there's no need to be so high-handed!" the man protested.

"I'm sorry," I said again. "But I won't have the Priory littered with bags and bottles. I'm responsible for its safe-keeping, and——"

I turned slightly and saw another, hitherto unnoticed figure standing quietly on the cloister garth, and my heart gave a great leap. For it was Ifor Williams standing there, wearing town clothes, and obviously taking in every word.

I know I blushed all over my face and neck, and I would gladly have sunk through the grass. Ifor Williams! And I had been ranting and raving, once again calling someone ill-mannered.

The others had noticed him, too, and perhaps they thought he had something to do with the Priory, for they immediately capitulated. The father gave the eldest boy a push and said:

"Get that stuff picked up, son. We'll go on to Rhyl, and you can do what you like on the beach."

Ifor Williams crossed to me, where I stood in the nave, and I saw that his face was quite grave, with no sign of the sardonic amusement I had hated so much.

"Good work!" he said casually. "You certainly let them have it, and I hate litter-louts myself."

I was still speechless. I had dreaded our meeting, wondering what on earth I could say, but I had never imagined that it would happen at a moment when I was so little able to cope with things.

He went on:

"Gwenfron asked me to call with a message. I'm just off to Liverpool, and she's going to do the milking, as the men are rounding up the sheep. But she says she can be free by half past five if you'd like to go out cycling. She thought you might like to go up the Dee Valley toward Corwen."

"Oh!" I gasped. "Yes. Yes, I would."

"Well, she's going to be outside the post office about twenty to six. And don't worry about that lot. They'll be much happier in Rhyl, indeed they will."

"That lot" were already streaming away to their shooting brake, still leaving a gleam of glass and the cigarette pack and several matches in the middle of the garth.

"My car isn't in the way," he said. "I'll let them get away first."

There were a dozen things I might have said. That I hoped *Death of the Dragon* would be a success in Liverpool, that I was sorry I had called him ill-mannered . . . I thought of them all later. But all I could say at the time was "Thank you."

He nodded and went off, and I heard the Ford following the shooting brake along the narrow road.

Left alone, I put the tea tray on the wall near the front door, then automatically picked up the glass and the cigarette pack. I put my hands to my cheeks and found them still burning hot, and my knees felt weak. I plumped myself down on a sun-warmed stone and looked about me, feeling the silence once more sweeping back over the ancient place.

My Priory! It had suddenly seemed so, when I saw it being treated so badly. I realized with blank astonishment that I had really minded; that I had grown to appreciate the grace and peace of the place and deeply cared that no stone should be displaced by wanton carelessness.

Another thing I realized was that I didn't dislike Ifor Williams any more. Perhaps I never had, once I had learned that he had written *Death of the Dragon*. How *could* one dislike so unreasonably a man who had written one moving and splendid thing and might write others? Who was quite obviously a hundred times superior to oneself?

And he had approved of me at our third meeting—he would probably have done the same himself. But I had behaved like an idiot schoolgirl, not finding anything to say. And suddenly, passionately, I wanted him to know that I wasn't shallow and silly and altogether ignorant. Only how was he ever to know? I had started badly, and now I should probably never be able to be natural with him. In any case, I should soon be going away.

Two evenings later I was cycling along to Llanbryn Farm to have supper when I passed Ifor Williams standing outside the post office. He was talking to Olwen Jones, or rather she was talking to him. She was standing on her absurdly high heels, looking up at him, and her face was more animated than I had ever seen it.

I shot past as quickly as I could, just saying a brief "Good evening!" and as I went on I felt curiously ruffled. What in the world was the matter with me? Olwen Jones could talk to anyone she pleased, and it had nothing to do with me. Everyone seemed to admire Ifor Williams, and if Olwen wanted to smile up into his eyes, that had nothing to do with me, either.

But I still felt unsettled as I cycled along the sunlit valley, so peaceful and beautiful on that May evening. The hawthorn was by then in full flower, foaming over every hedgerow, and the air was so sweet that it pulled at my heart. Bird song, and evening fragrance, the rippling of the river, the light on the hills . . . It was all perfect. But, strangely, it made me sad and suddenly very lonely.

A disturbing suggestion

It was not until Friday that I had a letter from Llanrwst. I took it from the postman eagerly, sure that it meant that "Maggie" would come. But when I opened it I found that I had been too optimistic. Signing herself "Maggie Trevor," Aunt Mair's friend explained that she had been very ill herself, and certainly couldn't think of coming to the Priory for at least two months. When she was better she was going to stay with her daughter at Festiniog, and it would probably be a long visit. She was deeply sorry to hear of her old friend's accident, and hoped she would soon be better. Meanwhile, she was sure I would find someone else to look after the Priory. She ended with the remark that she was writing to Aunt Mair at the hospital.

So that was that. My only hope gone. Well, I should just have to write to the Society and tell them that they must find a temporary custodian. But first I must tackle the Sister and find out just how long Aunt Mair was likely to be in the hospital. Time was passing. It was already a fortnight since I had left London. I had promised Penelope that I would be away only three weeks, and then we would begin with rearranging the apartment and I would start job hunting.

I had several visitors early on Friday afternoon and couldn't get away to the hospital, but I telephoned and sent a message to Aunt Mair that I would be there on Saturday. When I went she seemed much brighter, and I felt very relieved. But she was still in pain and had also been having all sorts of tests for the high blood pressure. She clutched my hand and said how grateful she was to me for staying on. She seemed to think I was likely to stay indefinitely, and I longed to tell her that I would be gone in a week, but it had still been emphasized that she must on no account be worried. Perhaps the best thing to do would be to fix it up with the Society and tell her at the last moment, when she might be stronger. She had had quite sufficient shock in learning of her old friend's illness.

Afterward I cornered Sister Dunn and begged to be told the truth. How long would Aunt Mair be away from home?

She looked at me sympathetically.

"My dear, it will almost certainly be another couple of months, but no one can say definitely. For one thing, her leg will bother her for some time, and she could never cope with the sort of place you describe. So many stairs, for instance. I think what will happen is that, when she's discharged from here, she'll be sent to a convalescent home for a while. Do you have to go back to London?"

"Why, yes, of course," I said in surprise, for I thought she had realized there was no doubt about that. "And I should go by next Saturday at the latest. I'll have to make some arrangements quickly."

"You're looking very well," she said, smiling kindly. "Wales evidently suits you!"

"But I've got things to do in London," I said, and walked away in rather a disturbed frame of mind to have my usual café tea. Tomorrow I would write to the Society, which had its headquarters in Bangor, and ask if someone could come and see me as soon as possible. I must make it quite clear, at the very beginning, that they would have to find someone who would be willing to take over the Priory.

That evening Gwenfron and I walked on the hills and I poured out my problem.

"Aunt Mair will be upset, I'm afraid, but she can't expect me to stay here forever."

"It is difficult," Gwenfron agreed sympathetically. "But she'll understand, and they're sure to be able to find a temporary custodian. I suppose you're longing to get back to London?"

I should have answered with a fervent, "Yes, of course!" But suddenly, inexplicably, I found myself hesitating for a moment.

"Y-yes. Penelope expects me, and I must get a job. This was only meant to be a holiday."

Gwenfron gave me a long, thoughtful look.

"I know you couldn't bear to live in the country."

I stared back at her, struck by her tone.

"I don't suppose I ever shall, but it isn't nearly as bad

as I thought. Of course, the weather's been lovely lately, and that must make a difference. But still——"

"You find that there are things you like?"

"Oh, yes," I agreed. "I like the Priory, and most of the people, and, do you know, I'm trying to learn Welsh. I got the radio fixed and I listen to the Welsh programs. I do know a little already; just a few words. And I like the flowers—I suppose one should learn the names?—and the birds, and having animals. Dai's beginning to accept me a bit, I think. He actually put his head on my knee this morning when I was having my breakfast. And Blackie's heaven! I could watch him all day; he's so graceful and such fun. We could never have animals in our apartment."

"I know you like the Priory," she said. "Ifor told me about the litter and the way you dragged those two boys apart when they were fighting in the church."

I felt myself blushing and wished I'd outgrow the childish, embarrassing habit.

"I didn't know he was there until afterwards."

"He thought you did the right thing. People shouldn't be allowed to behave like that. Catrin, why do you avoid Ifor?"

The question was so unexpected that it took my breath away.

"I—I don't."

"I think you do. You don't seem to want to meet him around the farm, and you ask me down to supper instead of coming up when he's at home. Don't you like him?"

"He wrote *Death of the Dragon*," I said with difficulty. "It makes him seem not quite real, or else too real, I don't know which. And he must think me a silly thing, not knowing anything about the country—having such wrong ideas."

"Did he laugh at you?" she asked shrewdly. "Oh, but Ifor laughs a lot. I told you how he teases my Chester aunt about being afraid of cows. It doesn't mean much. He thinks you're very brave to tackle the Priory alone. He said so. Catrin, do you have to go away?"

Once more I gaped at her.

"Of course I do. How can I stay? I have to get a job."

"But if you stayed it would *be* a job. The Society would pay you, and you'd have no rent to pay or anything. Just for two or three months, until your aunt is quite well again. You'd have the summer in the country, and be here for the International Eisteddfod, and I'd help you to learn Welsh——"

"But it's impossible!" I said wildly, sinking down onto a cushiony bank of bilberries. "Penelope expects me, and I've never confessed that I'm here alone."

"You'd have to do that, of course, and I suppose it would be hard on Penelope——"

"She's used to living alone," I said, still rather stunned. "It was I who suggested living with her, though she seemed awfully pleased. Oh, no, Gwenfron!"

"I just wondered if you'd thought of it," she said placidly. "You'll do what you think best, of course."

I lay there on the bilberries, seeing only the blue sky and breathing the sweet smell of the hills.

It was odd that it had never struck me that I might stay on in Wales. At first my only thought had been to get away from Nant Gwyncefn, and then, when I began to like it, I still remembered constantly that it was only an interlude. If I stayed I might, sometime, get to know Ifor better, if only I could get over my idiotic, tongue-tied shyness. . . . I could see full summer . . . learn Welsh . . . and be there when the Red Dragon of Wales flew with dozens of other flags over Bishop Trevor's old stone bridge in the town.

"No," I said after a long time. "I hadn't thought of it. But it isn't possible."

Gwenfron said no more, and we walked on discussing modern music, but the disturbing seed had been sown. I had thought that I had only one problem now—how soon I could find someone to take my place at the Priory—but suddenly I had another. But it wasn't a problem at all, I told myself as we separated, Gwenfron to climb to the farm, and I to approach the Priory gates. Of course I wouldn't stay.

It was an exquisite evening. The sky was still stained flame and orange and brilliant blue, and a sharp young moon hung over the hills. The white hawthorn hedges gleamed in the gathering dusk, and the great limestone cliff, with the clear sky above it, looked like the backdrop to some ballet or opera. I unlocked the gates and stood in the middle of the cloister garth. There was an early star caught in the tracery of the rose window, and the church looked wonderful; the glorious arches in that magic dusk looked more beautiful than I had ever seen them. Or else I was seeing them with new eyes. The wallflowers growing among the stones sent out a sweet fragrance, and the black cats flitted about like ghosts, their green eyes shining.

Through one of the nave arches I could see lights

springing up in Gwyncefn Farm, and I imagined them all in the room with the carved fireplace and the harp: Mrs. Williams, Gwenfron, and Ifor. And soon I should be far away and never see any of them again.

Another person I should miss was Mr. Jones, with his friendly dark face and lilting voice. But I shouldn't mind not seeing Mrs. Jones and Olwen again. They didn't like me, I was sure of that, and I didn't care for them, but . . . Oh, well, I wouldn't think of them on such a lovely night.

Was it really only two weeks since I had been in such terror, imagining all sorts of nameless horrors as darkness fell? Would I really even mind now in wild wind and rain, or in snow? For some totally unknown reason that gave me a sharp stab of pain. Someone had told me the valley was lovely in snow, and I had replied with no regret that I should never see it. How one altered!

Still, even if I did stay on for another couple of months I shouldn't see snow. But I should see the summer bracken on the hills, the fruit swelling in the little orchards, the lambs growing into sheep among the fading buttercups.

"Oh, don't be sentimental!" I told myself as I went indoors. "You're going back to London. You know you are."

But, instead of getting into bed, I stood by my window for a long time, facing the fact that if I really wanted to stay in the country the choice was mine.

The next morning I thought I must have suffered a sort of madness. Of course I was going back to London! I sat down after breakfast and wrote to the secretary of the Society and immediately afterward cycled to the post office and dropped the important letter into the box. So that was that! They would find someone else, and my strangely blank future would be clear again.

That fine May Sunday brought a number of visitors to the Priory, all, fortunately, well behaved, and I was kept very busy showing them around. It had begun to please me very much to tell them the story of Gwyncefn and to point out the beauties of the Norman remains and the transition to Early English and Perpendicular. If only the cloisters had been spared, I sometimes told them, the Perpendicular vaulting would have been the finest in Wales.

I sometimes took people who seemed particularly interested down into the cellarium, and even showed them one or two of the rooms in the tower. After all, Aunt Mair had said that she sometimes took visitors, and who knew if some of these people might not like to come and stay for a night occasionally?

I did not, however, expect to have to cope with that myself. But on Monday morning there was a card from someone who signed himself "John Mayther." He said that he and his friends were taking an early holiday that week and were already in Wales. Would Mrs. Davies put them up as usual for a couple of nights? The four of them would arrive on Tuesday, and hoped it was all right.

Well, what could I do? I began to fly around preparing the two lowest tower rooms. If the four couldn't, or wouldn't, share double beds I would have to think again. I hadn't the slightest idea if they were four men, or two married couples, or what. I then went into town and bought as many provisions as I could carry, and, on my return, called in to ask Mrs. Jones to order extra meat from the butcher.

She took the order and then looked at me with her sharp dark eyes.

"So you're still here, girl? More than two weeks it iss!"

"Yes, I'm still here," I agreed casually. "But I'll probably be gone by next week end. Aunt Mair won't be back for about two months, but I've asked the Society to find someone else to take my place."

"You'll be fery glad to get back to London," she said, nodding her head almost with satisfaction. "No doubt you are finding the country fery dull indeed."

I might have said that I was too busy to find the country dull and that, in any case, I was enjoying the heavenly weather, but I didn't. I smiled and hurried back to the Priory to give Dai and the cats a meal and to finish preparing the guest rooms.

In the late afternoon I was weeding the flower beds at one side of the cloister garth and singing at the top of my voice when Gwenfron suddenly appeared at my side. I stopped singing very abruptly, feeling rather self-conscious, and she cried at once:

"Oh, Catrin! And you never told me!"

"What?" I asked, patting the earth around a clump of daisies.

"That you had such a lovely voice and could sing in Welsh."

"Is it lovely?" I asked in some surprise. I liked singing, and had been in the school choir during my last year, but I had never thought much of my voice.

"Of course it is. So strong and pure. And you were singing 'Men of Harlech' in Welsh. I had no idea——"

"Mother used to sing Welsh songs to me when I was a child," I explained. "I only know a few properly: 'Harlech' and 'David of the White Rock' and 'All Through the Night.' I don't know much Welsh, as I told you. And I'd far rather listen to *you* sing!"

Gwenfron plumped herself down on the grass.

"Oh, Catrin, if you were staying you could join the valley choir. We're always short of people, and with the Eisteddfod coming in July——"

I sat back on my heels and stared at her. Because I still remembered sometimes that I might have stayed, my voice was perhaps unnecessarily sharp.

"I can't stay just to sing in the choir!"

"Oh, of course not. But if——"

"Anyway, I've written to the Society to ask them to find someone else quickly. So it's too late."

Gwenfron hugged her knees, her eyes on the hills above the Priory arches.

"Oh, dear! I *am* sorry! I shall miss you, Catrin. There aren't many girls of my own age here. In fact, only Olwen Jones, and I've never had much in common with her. Besides, Mother doesn't like her at all, and she doesn't come to the farm."

Suddenly I knew that I should miss Gwenfron, too. I liked her so much, and we were rapidly slipping into a pleasant, unquestioning friendship.

"I'll miss you, of course—all of you. But, after all, it's been a good experience."

"Well, come to supper tonight, anyway, and we'll have

some music. Perhaps they won't find anyone to take your place."

"Oh, I don't suppose there'll be any difficulty," I said.

That night I climbed the lane to the farm, and Gwenfron met me by the white gate. As we walked through the garden Ifor suddenly joined us, and I felt a moment of sheer panic. So he was going to be there all evening, and I would have my chance to talk like an intelligent human being!

But after a brief greeting his first words were:

"I'm very sorry, but heaven knows when I shall get in to supper. I've got a cow on the point of calving, and it's a first calf."

"Oh, poor Blodwen!" cried Gwenfron. "Will she be all right?"

"Oh, I suppose so. But I'll stay with her. You'll excuse me, Catrin?"

"Of course," I said, not sure whether to be disappointed or relieved.

"Gwenfron says you're leaving soon."

"At the week end, I expect," I explained. And then, with difficulty: "I—I so admired *Death of the Dragon*. I saw it twice, and it really made me come to Wales. If you have another play I hope Gwenfron will let me know."

He paused with his hand on the gate that led to the farmyard, and once again his face was perfectly serious.

"They've got my second play now at the Royal Crown. It's called *Penillion** for David Evans*. I expect to hear any day."

* *Penillion* (pronounced Pen-i'thon) is a Welsh word for an ancient, traditional type of singing.

"And we'll all die of disappointment if they don't do it," said Gwenfron.

"Coming along to see Blodwen before you have supper?" Ifor asked carelessly, and we followed him slowly toward the cowsheds. The black and white mother-to-be was alone, for the rest of the herd was out in the fields. She lowed as we approached, and her big, soft eyes were troubled. She didn't look fierce or alarming, but somehow lovable.

Gwenfron stroked her between the horns, murmuring in Welsh, and Ifor leaned against the wooden partition in a casual, oddly graceful attitude. Suddenly he and his sister were very much alike, lost as they both were in sympathetic contemplation of the cow.

It was very quiet and rather shadowy in the building but, through the windows, I could see the sunlit fields by the river, where the shadows of the hills had not reached.

"Will she be long?" Gwenfron asked, and her brother said:

"Probably not. I hope we'll be able to show Catrin the new arrival before she goes home."

At supper Mrs. Williams talked about music and the theater, asking my opinion of some current plays that I had seen, and afterward Gwenfron went to the harp.

"Mother, Catrin can sing in Welsh. Imagine it! And she's been pretending to be such an outsider. Catrin, you shall sing 'Men of Harlech' for Mother."

"I'd far rather you did," I protested, but she smiled and ran her long, well-shaped fingers over the taut strings.

An hour later we were still singing, Gwenfron teaching me the Welsh words of "Land of Our Fathers," when I realized suddenly that Ifor was there. His dark hair was on end and he looked tired.

"I thought our unalterable rule was 'No farm boots in the house'!" Mrs. Williams said mildly.

"Indeed it is. But I came to call the girls. I didn't realize you were having a concert."

"Is the calf born?" Gwenfron demanded, springing up, and he nodded.

"A well-marked little creature—female."

Out we went into the cooling evening air and across the yard to the cowshed. Anxiety had gone, and Blodwen was contentedly licking a surprisingly large black and white calf. It had very long legs and the most melting eyes.

"It's like a miracle!" I cried, astonished to find myself almost unbearably moved by the peaceful scene. I suppose that country children are used from the earliest age to the birth of animals, but I had never seen such a young creature. Before supper it had not been there, and now it was making frantic efforts to rise on those long legs, while Blodwen pushed it with her nose.

Gwenfron offered to walk back with me, but I said I would be quite all right alone. I was unexpectedly, warmly happy as I walked down the lane, remembering the newborn calf and the way Ifor Williams had looked. He had written what was perhaps a great play, but he still cared about the farm. I had forgotten to be shy or afraid of him as we stood in the cowshed, though I certainly had not had an opportunity of talking intelligently.

"This time next week I shall be in London, and it will all seem quite unreal," I told myself.

‡ɑ‡ɑ 9 ɒ‡ɒ‡

Visitors at the Priory

John Mayther had not said what time he and his friends would arrive, so I did not like to go far away on Tuesday morning. After I had done my housework I knelt in the nave, clipping the edges of the grass with a pair of shears. Once again it was a lovely day, and I wondered how much longer the good weather could last.

Bledig had long since forgotten to be dignified with me, and, as he did his best to climb onto my sloping "lap," I wondered how I had ever thought him a cold and inscrutable animal.

"You can't settle there!" I cried, pushing him off gently. "I'm moving along all the time, and I'm kneeling. It's not a proper lap."

Bledig then sat down immediately in front of me, so that I couldn't move the shears without cutting him to pieces. I picked him up, kissed the top of his shining head, and dumped him behind me.

"I'm sure I hope you'll be well looked after when I go," I said as Dai arrived with a large, much-chewed bone and settled himself not far away, his eyes on me. Now we were friends, and he welcomed me with enthusiasm if I'd only been away for an hour. It was going to be hard to have to leave him.

My meditations, and the gentle movement of the shears, were interrupted by the sound of bicycle bells and cheerful laughter, and when I looked around a pillar there were four young people just dismounting at the side of the cloister garth—two young men and two girls of about my own age, all in shorts and bright shirts or blouses.

My visitors! I threw down the shears and followed Dai across the grass. The dog, after a preliminary cautious sniff, was greeting them as old friends, and they made a fuss over him, ruffling his soft fur.

They looked at me in surprise, and I said quickly:

"Aunt Mair—Mrs. Davies—is in the hospital. She had an accident. I'm in charge temporarily, and so——"

"Oh, I say!" the taller of the young men cried concernedly. "I am sorry. We always look forward to seeing her. I wrote, but of course you wouldn't want—— We can go somewhere else, I suppose."

"There's no need to," I said. "The rooms are ready, though I didn't know how many beds you'd want. And the butcher comes today, so you won't starve."

"The girls generally sleep in the bottom tower room and we farther up," John Mayther said. "This is Bill, and these are Carrie and Margaret. Do you really mean it? We'd be awfully grateful! We love the Priory. We spent last night at a hostel, but——"

"I've done those rooms, so you can go up," I said, wondering what Millicent would say if she could see me being a landlady. It was rather fun, especially as I liked their looks so much.

It continued to be fun, for they were obviously used to being very much at home. After lunch John and Bill insisted on doing odd jobs, such as mending the shed door and oiling the lawnmower, while the girls sun-bathed in a corner, against the wall of the chapter house.

When I went to sit with them I found them very envious of my sojourn in the Priory.

"We'd love to look after it. It's so beautiful and interesting, isn't it? But you must find it very different from London."

"I did at first," I said, with shameful memories of my first nights of terror. "Yes, it's a fascinating place. But I'm leaving very soon. In fact, I thought someone from the Society might come and see me today. I wrote and told them they must find someone else."

"We've only taken a week's holiday, or we'd take it on for a while," Carrie said longingly. "Give me the country every time! We work in Liverpool, you know."

The afternoon passed and still there was no sign of anyone from Bangor. There should at least have been a letter, and I felt a little disturbed. Well, perhaps tomorrow——

"There's a dance in Corwen tonight," John said as we carried our tea out of doors. "We heard about it last night and thought we might cycle along there. Apparently it was put off from Saturday. What about joining us?"

"Oh, but——" I was sorely tempted. I loved dancing. "You're even numbers——"

"Don't worry about that. We never stick together, anyway, at these affairs. Do come."

By the time we were ready, I wearing a pretty blue dress, it was another perfect evening. As we cycled along the Dee Valley the scene was absolutely idyllic: the peaceful hills, the shining river, the meadows beginning to be golden with buttercups. And the dance, in a small church hall, was fun.

My companions, though entirely English, seemed to have no difficulty in making themselves at home in Wales, and for my part I realized, as I waltzed with a young Welshman, that I felt less of a stranger. I could even understand a few snatches of Welsh conversation. And yet there was still the faintly exciting feeling that I was in a foreign land, a land where the faces and voices were by no means familiar.

It grew very hot, but I enjoyed every moment, never lacking partners.

"Come again," said the young Welshman who had claimed me several times. "Fery glad we are to see some new faces. Come and fetch you on my motorcycle, I will, if you just say the word."

"I can't," I said. "Though I'd like to. I'm going back to London very soon."

"Stay you in Nant Gwyncefn," he said. "Better than old London any time. Too many people in London; nefer get to know them all!"

As we cycled back through the moonlight and starlight

I thought how often I would remember my various experiences, and it would at least be fun to tell Penelope all about them. She was always such a good listener.

But in the morning the postman brought a letter from Penelope. I read it as I watched the coffee.

"Dear Catrin,

"Well, how are you enjoying Wales? Thanks for your card giving the address. Are you spending the whole time with your aunt, then? Thought you were going adventuring. But Millicent seemed relieved when I met her the other day. I know that she and your father weren't really keen on your wanderings in Wild Wales.

"Look, Catrin, don't hate me too much. I'm frightfully sorry, but I just can't refuse. The firm wants me to go to Paris for six or eight weeks, and I've said I will. So the sharing of the apartment will have to wait for a little while. I'll send you the key to Sloane Street, and you can get started with putting in your things, of course. And good luck with the job. I'm sure you'll get one quickly.

"Write soon to say you forgive me, but I expect I may see you before I go, as you said you'd only be away three weeks. I'm off a week from Friday."

I let the coffee boil over and the toast burn. Lucky Penelope, to be going to work in Paris! But I was dismayed to learn that our plans for living together had been deferred. Of course, two months would soon pass quickly, but I had imagined myself moving in very soon. I didn't really want to have to stay on at home, especially now that I had tasted independence. The thought crossed my mind that I might, after all, have stayed in Wales, but I dismissed it. The decision had been taken, and probably some other arrangement was already being made. But why hadn't the Society's secretary answered my urgent letter?

My visitors went off to spend the day walking on the hills, and I locked the Priory and went to do my shopping in Llangollen. I cycled, as the buses were so inconvenient, and on my return, when only about half a mile from the Priory, I was passed by a small, shabby car.

"A visitor!" I thought, and pedaled faster. When I reached the gates the middle-aged man was smoking a cigarette and studying the old bell and rope. He turned as I dismounted.

"Miss Drury?"

"Yes," I said, unlocking the padlock and swinging wide the gates. "I'm sorry to have kept you waiting, but I had to do some shopping. Do you want to see——?" And then I realized that his use of my name meant only one thing.

"I represent the Society, Miss Drury. You wrote and explained the situation, and I may say that I'm very sorry to learn that Mrs. Davies is in the hospital." He followed me onto the cloister garth and looked all around, and I was glad that the grass was so well cut and the flower beds in such good order. There wasn't even a carelessly flung match to mar the scene. I felt curiously like a proud parent having her child inspected.

"Hum! What a very beautiful spot this is! I need hardly say that we're very grateful to you for carrying on here. I hadn't thought you'd be so young, my dear."

"I'm older than I look," I said firmly. "And I've enjoyed it. I suppose you've come to tell me that you've found someone to take over. I do hope they'll be willing to look after the dog and the cats——"

He shook his head. He had a pleasant appearance: a Welsh face and slightly graying, very crisp hair.

"By the way, I should have told you that my name's Morgan. No, I'm afraid we haven't found anyone. It isn't easy to find custodians for such lonely places these days. People like electricity and 'all mod. con.,' as they say."

"Oh!" I stared at him, and he stared back consideringly.

"You wouldn't agree to stay on here until Mrs. Davies is better? We aren't able to pay much, but we might come to a satisfactory arrangement——"

My cheeks flushed and my heart felt as though a load had rolled off it. I could stay, after all! I could make it my job for a little while and not have to leave Dai and the cats in someone else's hands! I could——

I remembered Millicent and my father and realized that I ought to consult them. How on earth would they feel when they heard the full story?

"I—I don't know," I said. "In a way I'd like to, just for a few more weeks. I love the Priory and would take very good care of it. But it's not as easy as all that."

"You said you wanted to get back to London."

"Well, I ought to go back. But things have altered a little since I wrote to you——"

In the end, over a cup of tea, he persuaded me to stay on for another week before letting them know definitely whether I would take on the job. Meanwhile, I would be paid for the time I had been there, and Aunt Mair shouldn't suffer.

"She's been a very faithful guardian of these ruins," Mr. Morgan said appreciatively. "And we'll see she's all right, though we're not a rich Society. Telephone me as soon as you've made up your mind, Miss Drury."

I promised, and, after giving him the money I had collected from visitors and asking for some more guidebooks, I walked with him to his car.

The moment he had gone bumping away up the lane I did a wild little jig, much startling Dai, who barked and capered around me. The relief was really surprising to me. I simply hadn't known that I minded so much the thought of going away, until I had a chance to revoke the decision.

But I soon grew more sober, and after a quick lunch I settled down to write that difficult letter to my father and Millicent. I had to confess that I had been at the Priory alone and make them see that it was all right to stay. The letter took me a long time, but I was satisfied with it in the end and took it to the post office.

Mrs. Parry, the thin little postmistress with the shrill voice, smiled at me across the counter as I bought stamps.

"I hear you're leafing us soon. Indeed, that will be a pity."

"Perhaps I'm not, after all," I said cheerfully. "The Society wants me to stay on until Aunt Mair's better."

"And you can tell that to Mrs. Jones and Olwen!" I added to myself as I cycled back to the Priory. I had learned early in my stay that anything said to Mrs. Parry was soon all over the valley. She was a gossip, but a kindly one, and I liked her very much.

I prepared a huge supper for my visitors when they returned from their day on the hills, and we had a merry meal, followed by singing out on the garth. Gwenfron joined us, and we sang until the shadows of the ruins crept all the way across the grass.

"I may stay here, after all," I said to Gwenfron as I saw her off. "I think I'm almost sure to, because Penelope's going to Paris for a few weeks and Mr. Morgan from the Society can't find anyone else. But I've got to hear what Father and Millicent will say."

"Oh, good!" she cried, and her eyes immediately lighted up. "We'd be so glad. And I've got news, too. I didn't want to say anything in front of the others. Ifor's new play is almost certain to be put on at the Royal Crown, and, do you know, a British film company just *may* want to buy the film rights of *Death of the Dragon*."

"But that's wonderful!" I gasped. "Please tell your brother how glad I am." Immediately my mind ran ahead and I saw myself back in that familiar theater, once more under the spell of Ifor Williams's compelling prose. How strange it would be to have met him; to know what he looked like! "But when will the play be put on?"

"Oh, not until the autumn at the very earliest. You'll be back in London by then."

But the autumn seemed so far away that I could not visualize it at all.

The next morning the four young people departed, with a promise from me that, if I was still there, they could come back for a week end soon. I told myself that *if* I stayed—and my mind was made up about that—I might occasionally take other people. If ever I grew lonely that would be the solution, and it would be a little extra money toward my savings.

The day passed peacefully, my only visitors being Idwal and Inigo Jones from the inn. I had not seen very much of them since my arrival in Nant Gwyncefn; only occasionally in the distance, playing in the river, riding their bicycles up and down the village, grinning rather shyly at me over the garden wall as I passed the Collwyn Arms. They were quite good-looking children, but I didn't take to them.

I was quite surprised to see the pair of them outside the front door, hands in pockets and their cheeks bulging with candy.

They had come, they said, to bring a message from their "mam." Would I like to visit the inn that evening?

I wasn't keen about it, but I didn't want to hurt anyone's feelings, and it was, of course, well known that I frequently went to Gwyncefn and Llanbryn Farms.

So about seven o'clock I went along to the Collwyn Arms and found that, in spite of the bright evening, Mrs. Jones and the two little boys were watching television in the sitting room. It wasn't nearly so nice as the kitchen, I thought, but Mrs. Jones seemed proud of the modern furniture, and once, when I had admired the old Welsh dresser, she shrugged and said:

"Well, indeed, that old thing! It belonged to my husband's mother. Give it away for nothing, I would, if he'd let me!"

Halfway through the program Olwen sauntered in and stretched herself out in one of the deep chairs, and when things were quiet in the bar Mr. Jones occasionally put his head around the door and watched for a few minutes. Nothing was said about my plans until Mrs. Jones, Olwen, the boys, and I were sitting down to supper, and then Mrs. Jones suddenly shot at me:

"Iss it true, girl, that you're thinking of staying on? 'I'll nefer believe it,' I said, 'until I hear it from her own lips. Fery anxious to get back to London, she iss.' "

"Yes," I said calmly. "It's quite true. The Society has asked me to, and I don't really need to go back to town just yet."

"Well, now!" Olwen exclaimed, with her fork halfway to her mouth. "And what's the great attraction? Nothing very much for a London girl in this valley that I can see!"

"The Priory is the attraction," I said coolly, disliking her quite a lot but determined not to show it. "And the fact that they can't find anyone else. Besides, I find I like the country."

"A-ah!" she said in a meaningful tone. She was wearing a bright-blue sleeveless sweater, very tight indeed, and a gray skirt that was also very tight. "So it's up to Gwyncefn Farm you'll be? There on Monday—— A little bird was telling me." Her tone was certainly not friendly.

I reacted to her meaning with a rush of anger, and wondered why I hadn't fully realized it before. She hated me to go to Gwyncefn Farm because I would probably meet Ifor Williams. She was jealous, though heaven knew she had no reason to be. Ifor Williams cared less than nothing for me, and I had scarcely said ten consecutive words to him.

"Fery stuck up they are at the farm," Mrs. Jones remarked.

I had ignored Olwen, but I couldn't ignore that.

"Oh, they're not! Gwenfron and her mother have been very kind to me."

"Stuck up, nefertheless! Oh, fery friendly Gwenfron iss on the surface, but nefer really one of us. Not that everyone would agree with me. Fery popular she iss with most people. But Mr. Williams now—there's the handsome one, and so clefer, but always a pleasant word. He and Olwen are fery good friends."

"How nice!" I said weakly. I couldn't think of another word to say. I remembered Olwen talking to Ifor by the post office, so smilingly intent. I changed the subject hastily by asking some question about the International Eisteddfod, and the conversation was more general until I rose to leave.

I told myself, as I cycled along the road under the shadowy trees, that I didn't want to go to the inn very often, especially when Mr. Jones was busy. I should never, never have anything in common with Olwen, and I didn't wonder at all that Mrs. Williams disliked her. My cheeks burned as I remembered her hints about the "attraction" in Nant Gwyncefn.

It wasn't Ifor Williams! Of course it wasn't! Though I would like to get to know him better and have some conversations about the theater.

The next day I went to see Aunt Mair and was lucky enough to get a lift back. I was just carrying my tea out onto the cloister garth when I heard a car drive up and stop. A couple of minutes later a small girl in an emerald dress, with sandals of the same color, ran through the gates, and there was something familiar about the fair curls and sturdy limbs.

"Delphine!" I shouted.

A woman followed, and I put down the tray with hands that were suddenly unsteady.

"Millicent!"

"Welcome to Wales!"

Delphine made such a fuss over me that it was some moments before I met Millicent's eyes again. She was standing quite calmly on the cloister garth, her observant gaze taking in every visible detail. But when our eyes met she said:

"Well, Catrin? I thought the best thing was to come, so I put a few things in a suitcase and left yesterday afternoon. Your father said he could do without the car for a few days, and we found a very good hotel last night. You're looking wonderfully well!"

"Oh, Millicent!" was all I could say, and she laughed.

"We've taken her by surprise, Delphine. Anyway, a cup of tea will be welcome. Can you find another cup? And a glass of milk for Delphine?"

"Of course," I said, galvanized into action, and I flew into the house. When I returned, Delphine was playing with Blackie and Millicent was sitting on a low block of stone against the wall of the chapter house, powdering her nose.

"It's certainly a charming spot—and I've never seen you look better. I always thought you looked peaky while you were at that commercial college. But let's not talk until I've had a first cup."

She drank her tea with evident enjoyment, while I quivered with anxiety. In my weeks of independence I had forgotten the effect that Millicent had on me. If I had to fight that calm assurance, how would it all end? With my going meekly back to London, no doubt. I was legally of an age to leave home, but I didn't want to quarrel or do anything to upset my father and stepmother.

"We were very much surprised," Millicent said presently. "That is, your father was. I had read something between the lines of your previous letters."

"You always were a witch!" I flashed at her, and she laughed in her rather restrained way.

"I know you, Catrin, and you sounded guilty. I was sure you were keeping something back. And you've really enjoyed being in charge here? I should have thought you'd hate every moment of it!"

"I did hate it at first," I told her. "I stayed only because I'd promised. But now I love the Priory, and there are so many people, and I'm learning Welsh. After all, I *am* half Welsh."

"I should have thought you wholly a Londoner," she remarked, a little amused. "You really confound me. Here you are, with a dog and three cats, and taking in visitors and showing people around. It's no life for a young girl!"

"But I do like it!" I protested, in fright. "And I go out

a lot in the evenings. Last night I was at the inn, and the other night I went to a dance at Corwen. And then there's Gwyncefn Farm. I told you about Gwenfron and her mother——"

"*And* the brother. Fancy a Welsh farmer writing plays! I didn't see *Death of the Dragon,* but I'm sure I'd have detested it. The Welsh never seem to me to have any sense of humor, and if English cities need water there's no point in making a song and dance—or rather, a play—about a few cottages being flooded."

"It was a wonderful play," I argued, up in arms. "And it *does* matter! Why should Welsh villages——?"

"Now, now, Catrin, I didn't come here to argue about Welsh affairs. You'll be telling me that you're a Welsh Nationalist next. It's enough that you're in Wales and that you want to stay in Wales. We both think it's fantastic, but your father's left it to me. Do show me the house."

I showed her every corner of it, thankful that it was as clean and tidy as possible, and I even displayed the tower and the cellarium with pride, though I knew that Millicent would not be impressed.

"What an extraordinary place!" she said frankly, holding Delphine firmly by the hand as we climbed the cellarium steps again. "But it all looks very clean. You must be a better housewife than I thought."

"I like it," I said defensively. "I like cooking, too. I just didn't know."

"You'll be making jam yet and bottling plums," my stepmother remarked. She didn't mean to be unkind; it was just her way.

"The plums won't be ready for months," I said, trying

to speak lightly. She always made me feel young and foolish.

"Well, you know what I mean. I suppose it isn't a bad
thing. When Penelope comes home from Paris you'll have
to cook for each other. I always wondered how you'd manage. But meanwhile——"

"Meanwhile——" I repeated anxiously. I didn't dare to
fight openly, but I felt both troubled and rebellious.

"It's fantastic, as I said. By the way, can you put us up?
You must be able to, surely, since you coped with four
young people. Delphine ought to go to bed early."

"Of course," I said. "I've plenty of food in the house,
and you can have Aunt Mair's room. I'll sleep in the
tower. It won't take more than a few minutes to change
the sheets."

"But you can't sleep in that place!"

"I can. I slept there for two nights when I first came,
and the visitors loved it. They always have the two lower
rooms, so they told me."

"Well, you've got some courage, I must say. But you'll
tire of this incredible place, and then where will you be?"

"Still here!" I said with a grin. "I *won't* tire, but if I do
I'll have to stay until Aunt Mair gets back."

"Perhaps she won't be able to manage things here
again. A broken hip at her age——"

"Oh, I think she will. The Sister said so."

"One never knows how these things will turn out,"
Millicent remarked. "She must be getting on in years——"

"Not much more than sixty," I said briskly, conscious
that my ideas had changed in that direction, too. I was
far more ready to accept people whatever their age; and

sixty no longer, for some reason, seemed as though it had one foot in the grave.

Delphine insisted that I should put her to bed and sing to her, and I sang Welsh songs softly until she was asleep. Looking at her, tucked up in the big bed, I realized that I had been missing my little half sister, and for the first time I wondered what my own children would be like when I had them.

But that was silly, when I wasn't even thinking of marrying and settling down, and I laughed to myself. Enough, at the moment, to deal with Millicent and get my own way about staying in Wales.

Millicent was appalled by the old-fashioned kitchen grate and the oil stove, and I very firmly got rid of her while I cooked the supper. She gave me an amused look and went to wander in the ruins, and somehow it seemed a minor victory, auguring well for the future.

Gwenfron arrived when we had nearly finished eating and looked startled to see Millicent. I introduced them a trifle shyly and soon saw with relief that Millicent approved of Gwenfron. At least *she* didn't write Welsh plays; a future career as a nurse was wholly admirable and showed a great deal of sense.

"What do *you* think about Catrin's staying on?" Millicent demanded with a shrewd glance at the thoughtful face opposite, and Gwenfron said promptly:

"I think it's a good idea, and so does Mother—now. At first we all thought Catrin wouldn't like the Priory; that she'd be lonely, being a town girl. But she's managed splendidly."

"Hum!" was all that Millicent said then, but when Gwenfron had gone, after having coffee with us, she remarked:

"A nice girl. You say they have money?"

"I didn't say so," I protested. "I said they own a great deal of the valley. But I don't think the farms bring in much rent, and Ifor works very hard. The house is lovely, but rather shabby. I shouldn't think there's a lot of money. But if Ifor gets his first play filmed——"

"People get ridiculously large sums for film stories," said Millicent.

No more was said about my staying, and I spent an anxious night, waking often to the remembrance of Millicent's presence.

Nothing was said at breakfast, either, and I was growing really bothered by the time Millicent, Delphine, and I wandered out into the ruins. Millicent had said that she meant to leave in the early afternoon, and time was getting short.

We were just entering the chapter house when I heard a car and turned back. A plump woman came toward me, smiling and holding out her hand.

"You must be Mrs. Davies's niece? Miss—Miss Drury, is it? Well, I'm Mrs. Emyrs Rhys-Jones, a member of the Eisteddfod Hospitality Committee. I'm arranging accommodation for the members of foreign choirs and dance teams who will be coming to town during the first week in July."

Conscious of Millicent listening in the background, I said doubtfully:

"Oh, yes?"

"And I hope——"

"But you know that my aunt is in the hospital?"

"Yes, my dear, and indeed we're all very sorry. But Mr. Jones at the Collwyn Arms told me that you were in charge, and he was sure you'd be willing to put up some people for me." She brought out a sheaf of papers. "Now, let me see. There will be a lot of Swiss. Dancers from an Alpine village and yodelers from Berne. How many could you take? Last year I think it was——"

I caught Millicent's eye. It was a slightly amused, slightly withdrawn eye, and somehow her expression gave me courage. I said with dignity:

"If they don't mind sharing double beds I could take six in the tower, and I might be able to clear another room. There are two small beds, but the rooms are full of old furniture. Say eight. But if my aunt is back and not very well——"

"Then of course I shall understand. But it's such a very romantic place, and foreigners always love it. Well, thank you very much indeed, and I'll let you know the exact numbers later." She smiled and went off, looking thoroughly busy and pleased with herself.

"Not content," said Millicent, "with all you've taken on already, you propose to cope with eight Swiss. And you can't even speak German!"

"I can a little," I said. "And oh, Millicent! It sounds like such a wonderful time! The world comes to Wales then. I couldn't bear to miss it."

"You can see the world in London any day of the week," she retorted, staring thoughtfully at the low, crouching house across the garth. "Well, I can see you're determined to stay, Catrin, so I'll say no more. But there's just one thing—— Promise you'll let us know if you're in any trouble. At once, mind!"

"I promise," I said. "Oh, Millicent——!"

"I'll tell your father that you're safe, happy, and able to manage things. But I'm not wholly happy myself, and I must admit that I don't understand you."

Well, that wasn't surprising, since my altered outlook was still strange even to me, and Millicent had never really understood me, in any case.

"I expect I take after Mother," I said, half to myself. "She loved the farm and the mountains, though she gave them up to live in London."

"Perhaps you're right," Millicent said briskly. "Anyway, I suppose you're old enough to know what you want."

"I hope so," I said soberly.

Then we talked about other things until lunchtime, and afterward Millicent put the luggage in the car and prepared to depart.

"We'll spend the night somewhere on the way and get started very early in the morning. I don't want to keep the car too long."

At the last minute I kissed her with unusual warmth.

"Good-by, Millicent, and thank you. You've been awfully decent."

"I hope I've been sensible," she said wryly. "But one can't stop girls growing up. Only don't get too Welsh, I beg of you, Catrin."

"Do you dislike the Welsh?" It was my turn to be amused.

"Well, not to say *dislike,* but they always seem so unnecessarily foreign. After all, it's England really, isn't it?"

"Don't say that to Mr. Jones or even Gwenfron," I said. "No, Millicent, Wales is a separate country and——"

Then Delphine tried to climb up me to kiss me good-by, and I hugged her for the last time.

"Good-by, poppet! When I come home I'll bring you a Welsh doll with a red cloak and a tall hat."

"Yes, please!" cried Delphine.

When they had gone I felt very strange for a short time. I had won! I was alone again, free to enjoy my own territory. For better or worse I had taken on the Priory, and for the next two or three months, my life would be bounded by a narrow Welsh valley.

"I must go and telephone Mr. Morgan!" I said aloud.

I decided to go into town to do some shopping, too, and I cycled all the way, enjoying the sun on my bare arms and legs. I stood on the bridge and looked down at the river and then up at the steep hills that enclosed the little town. A train stopped on its way to Ruabon, Wrexham, and Chester, and I watched it without any wistfulness. I wasn't going—I didn't want to go. Not yet, anyway.

I did my shopping with my thoughts still mainly on the momentous decision I had taken, and, making my last purchases at a shop opposite the station, set off rapidly toward the bridge again. The bridge at Llangollen is narrow, and there is usually a good deal of traffic on it, and of course I had to be in the very center of it when a slight bump sent a large package of cornflakes flying out of my overfilled basket.

I leaped off and reached for the box, while still trying to hold my bicycle upright, and a can of soup bounced into the roadway and rolled under the wheels of the hooting car behind me.

A passer-by retrieved the cornflakes for me, and, scarlet to the ears at the annoyance and amusement I was causing, I decided to go on without the soup. In no more than seconds I seemed to have created quite a sizable traffic jam. Feeling thoroughly silly, I was just going to mount when a voice shouted:

"Wait a minute, Catrin!"

Obediently, and with not the least idea who had called, I dragged my bicycle into one of the small embrasures, and the cars began to move again. Dodging between them came Ifor Williams, clutching my can of soup!

"Making an idiot of myself again!" I thought gloomily. "Though, really, this might happen to anyone."

"You seem to have a load," Ifor remarked as he reached me. "Let me take some of the things back for you. I've got the car in the car park."

"Oh, thank you, but I think I can manage. I'll just re-pack it a bit," I said, grateful to see that he looked perfectly grave. My two earliest meetings with Ifor Williams had made me, I suppose, ridiculously self-conscious.

"Are you in a hurry?"

"Yes. No. No, I'm not, really. I don't suppose there'll be any visitors."

"Then come and have some tea."

"Oh!" I gasped, rather taken aback and conscious that my hair was untidy.

"Don't look at me as though I'm the Red Dragon of Wales in person! We'll go to the Royal. Let me push your bike, and it will be quite safe against that wall."

I followed him meekly into the Royal Hotel, where a waiter who seemed to know him well immediately hurried off to fetch tea. Ifor offered me a cigarette, and I said awkwardly that I didn't smoke.

"Very sensible of you. It costs far too much." He sat there easily in a deep chair, with the bright light showing up his strongly marked face. One hand hung over the arm of the chair, and I noted with pleasure that it was well shaped and smoothly brown. It didn't look like the hand of a farmer, though the long fingers were capable enough.

He saw me looking at him and smiled, and I felt myself blushing. I would have given anything to be at ease with him, but I wasn't. It was a relief when the tea tray came and I could busy myself with the teapot and hot-water jug.

"Gwenfron says you're staying," he said as I handed him his cup and then offered the plate of sandwiches.

"Oh, yes. My stepmother's gone back now, and it's all settled with the Society. I'm glad."

His gaze was a trifle quizzical but not really amused. It even seemed sympathetic.

"Don't bite my head off, but I suppose I may take it that you now see something in country life?"

I swallowed a bite of tomato sandwich rather quickly. It was the moment that I had been expecting and slightly dreading. I turned to him and said:

"I was an idiot, and I don't blame you for laughing at me. I didn't know anything. I—I've been sorry about our first two meetings. You must have thought—have thought——"

"*You* thought me very rude about the cows," he said.

"And indeed I was, really. But if you'd seen yourself cling-ing to that hedge and looking so indignant! It wasn't fair to laugh, but I've often been in trouble for an overde-veloped sense of humor. 'Don't be sarcastic-funny!' Gwen-fron used to say when she was young. I'm really very sorry, and I think you've been exceedingly brave, taking on the Priory and living there alone."

I stared at him, suddenly warmed.

"I was scared stiff at first."

"Braver than ever, then. And look here! If you're ever in trouble and want help, ring the Priory bell—the one by the gate—several times. Say ten times and then another ten. Sound travels a long way in the valley, and we'd know——"

"I hope I shan't be in trouble——"

"So do I, but one never knows."

After that a silence fell and I sought wildly for things to say. The theater—— Thanks to my father, and to my friendship with Penelope, I knew quite a lot about the theater. Usually I could wax reasonably intelligent during a discussion, but, faced with the author of *Death of the Dragon,* I couldn't think of one single remark to make. I passionately wanted to show that I was not wholly igno-rant, but my mind was blank.

Ifor saved the situation by chatting casually about life in the valley and telling me that I must certainly join the Gwyncefn Choir and sing at the Eisteddfod.

"We meet for practice three times a week in the village hall now that the Eisteddfod's getting near. A week from Monday is the next one. Mr. Evans, the schoolmaster, is our conductor. Very musical he is." The last little turn of phrase reminded me sharply of Ifor's "Welshness." Mostly, like Gwenfron, there was no more than a slight lilt in his speech.

"But I can't really," I said in a panic. "Not sing at the Eisteddfod! I only know one or two songs in Welsh."

"You could manage well. In our section the songs are 'Jesu, Joy of Man's Desiring,' sung in Welsh, English, or German. We're singing it, of course, in Welsh. *Iesu, drud ddifyrrwch dynion.* Gwenfron could coach you in the words. Then 'David of the White Rock,' which you know, and a short original composition by Trefor Evans himself, which we've scarcely started to learn yet."

I was tempted, because I knew it would be exciting, as well as terrifying, to have even a small part in the great Eisteddfod, and to be included in the Gwyncefn Choir would make me feel that I belonged a little.

"Well, if you think it's all right."

"Of course. And Gwenfron's already told Mr. Evans. We're very short of female voices. Quite good our choir is, however. One year we came third. Not bad when there are so many entries."

I gave him a second cup of tea, and he began to talk about the sale of the film rights of *Death of the Dragon.* Apparently the deal had almost gone through, and, if all went well, the film would be made in the early spring of the next year.

"I shall be able to do a lot to the house and farm," he was saying thoughtfully, when a man who looked far more typically a farmer than Ifor Williams came up and began, after a few words to me, to talk about some cattle sale.

I sat there feeling curiously dreamlike. I was having tea

with Ifor Williams in a Welsh hotel, when a month ago I had never even imagined that I should get to know the author of *Death of the Dragon.* I didn't even resent the intrusion of the other farmer, for it gave me the opportunity to watch Ifor surreptitiously. It was odd how much his face and his hands and really everything about him were beginning to please me.

Soon after the other man had gone Ifor lit another cigarette and remarked:

"I suppose we ought to get back. I've got to see the shepherd."

"And I've got to cook the meat for Dai and the cats," I said, recalled to my housewifely duties.

"And you've got to cycle with that load. Are you sure you can manage?" He paid the waiter, and we wandered out into the sunshine side by side. There, walking past, was Olwen Jones, wearing a crisp white overall. Apparently she had just hurried out of the shop where she worked.

She said, "Hello!" and her face looked thoroughly unfriendly, I thought. But Ifor didn't seem to notice. He said, "Hello, Olwen!" cheerfully, and then turned to me again.

"Good-by, then, Catrin. And I'll see you at the choir practice, if not before. And—welcome to Wales, if it's not three weeks too late!"

Suddenly I was less stiffly shy. I grinned and said:

"That's what they have over the bridge during the Eisteddfod, don't they?"

"Of course. We welcome everyone then. But now you have a special little welcome for yourself." He smiled and nodded and hurried away to the car park, and I rather dazedly collected my bicycle and rode away, with the box of cornflakes still in a somewhat precarious position. I looked at it almost with affection. Without it I should not have had the opportunity of getting to know Ifor just a little better.

I was in high spirits that evening, even though the weather seemed to be changing at last. The wonderful sunlight of the past two or three weeks had made me feel that perhaps it would go on for a long time. But the weather forecast at six o'clock spoke of thunder, and then much colder, cloudier weather, and long before dark the air had grown unnaturally still and the world was heavy and gloomy.

It was eerie, but didn't really bother me, which just shows how much I had changed, or else how very high my spirits were.

Gwenfron didn't appear, but I didn't really mind. I settled down in the kitchen, accompanied by Dai and all three cats, and got on with my reading and my study of Welsh, Gwenfron having lent me a grammar a short while before.

It grew darker and darker, but no rain had fallen by the time I decided that I would go to bed early. I was suddenly very sleepy after my restless time the night before, worrying about Millicent's decision.

I had thought that perhaps I wouldn't bother to move from the tower for a while. It was a larger and airier room than Aunt Mair's, and the bed was exceedingly comfortable. So I made my way up there by lamplight—having got quite handy with the oil lamps by then—and Blackie followed me. He had definitely established himself as my nightly companion, though the other two liked to go out hunting. Dai preferred his bed in the kitchen, although he was free to wander about the house and up to the tower if he liked.

I put down the lamp on the old-fashioned chest of drawers and went to the window. It was quite early and should not have been dark, but the thundery gloom had deepened rapidly and I could only just glimpse the nearer arches of the church against the inky sky. No moon, no stars, though there were lights up at Gwyncefn. I could just see the farm if I craned my neck, and those lights were curiously warming.

"Once," I said to myself, "I should have been terrified. But even if it does thunder, the tower has stood for centuries, and there's no reason on earth why it should be struck by lightning."

Then, suddenly, I stiffened. The window was wide open, for the night was utterly airless, and I had heard a most extraordinary sound—a peculiar moaning that made my hair prickle on my scalp.

Blackie had heard it, too, for he was staring toward the window in a way that was not very reassuring, every whisker alert. He was a nervous, jumpy little cat at the best of times.

With the lamplight behind me, I couldn't really see anything, so I turned the wick very low and, with my flash in my hand, returned to the window. My heart was thumping, but beyond that I was really perfectly calm, and I noted the fact with relief. It didn't sound like any sort of owl; it was like a noise from another world.

It seemed to come from the eastern end of the church or from the north transept.

"Very superstitious they are in these parts!"

Well, they might be, but I wasn't, and I had learned to love and not to fear the Priory. All the same, it was very peculiar, and I didn't much care for it.

As I stood there at the window I suddenly saw a faint blue light moving near the place where the high altar had once been, below the great east window. It leaped about in the strangest way, and my blood did start to run rather coldly.

After all, there wasn't a soul nearer than the inn or Gwyncefn Farm, and the thundery night made my situation seem all the more solitary. Was it even remotely possible that the Priory was haunted, after all?

Mystery at the Priory

"Rubbish!" I said aloud. "It can't be!" And I made for the door, using my flashlight. I was partly undressed, having washed in the kitchen, but that didn't deter me. There was an old coat of Aunt Mair's hanging in the passage that led to the front door, and I put it on as I called Dai. He came looking rather sleepy and unwilling, but when I opened the door he followed me out onto the garth.

There was an odd hissing sound, which I soon realized was the noise of heavy raindrops. The moaning had stopped, and I could see no sign of the blue light. Everywhere was very dark, very silent—except for the rain—and decidedly uninviting.

"Good dog!" I said. "Go and find! Go on, Dai!"

Dai looked at me intelligently in the light from my flash and bounded off toward the church. He was back in a couple of minutes, wagging his tail and looking perfectly happy, and by then I had retreated to the doorway out of the increasing downpour. He shook himself all over Aunt Mair's coat and then ran back to the kitchen, with every appearance of having done his duty.

Much puzzled, I shut and locked the door again. But I was relieved, too. No dog would, surely, look so normal in the presence of the supernatural?

I followed him back to the kitchen and saw that he had gone back to his bed.

Standing by the dying fire, I pondered the mystery. Perhaps the queer noise had been an owl, after all, though owls didn't show blue lights. For if there had been anyone there, Dai would have discovered him. He was a good watchdog and always suspicious of strangers. In any case, the outer gates of the Priory were shut and firmly bolted, and the whole place would be pretty difficult of access by any other way. The walls were high and there was barbed wire on the lower stretches, not to mention a tangle of undergrowth on the outer side in most places—bushes and brambles and rapidly growing nettles.

I thought of Millicent and wondered what she would say. She was the last person to be nervous, but she hadn't really liked my being alone in the Priory. Anyway, she didn't know and I hadn't the faintest thought of telling her.

Grimly I marched back up the tower stairs, and by then the rain was falling in torrents and there was another kind of blue light flickering about the ruins—the lightning. Once more I stood at the window, and in the next flash I could see the whole of the nave, and it was quite empty.

So I went to bed, thinking that I was in for another

disturbed night. But the thunder only kept me awake for
about a quarter of an hour, and after that I slept dreamlessly until eight o'clock on a gray and soppingly wet
morning.

I didn't mention the mysterious happenings to Gwenfron or anyone else, for in the light of day I thought that
I must have imagined them, or that they were capable of
some perfectly normal explanation. And nothing more
happened for several nights.

In spite of the wet weather I was perfectly happy, and,
in fact, that was another revelation to me. I had thought
that the country in bad weather must be terrible, but,
strangely, it wasn't. The mist wreathed over the hills, hiding most of the valley, the river was higher than it had
been since my arrival in Wales, and the lane was full of
puddles. But the air was surprisingly sweet, and when
Gwenfron and I walked the hill paths in the mist I found
a sharp pleasure. The drops clung to the bright green
bracken and to our hair, and our heavy shoes made a
squelching sound on the grassy tracks. Sheep darted away
from us as we approached, and there was an exciting feeling of being in an unknown world.

Gwenfron seemed to know every path and sheep track
on the hills, and there was not really the slightest danger
of our getting lost, though she was careful to keep us away
from the top of the limestone cliff that ended Nant Gwyncefn and also from the odd quarries scattered here and
there.

We walked on and on, past dark little mist-wreathed
fir woods and dimly seen farms, and came down at last

into the Dee Valley, where the river tumbled on its way to Chester and the distant sea.

"I've loved it," I said as we parted. "I just never knew——"

Gwenfron grinned, leaning against a wet gate at the foot of the lane that led to Gwyncefn Farm.

"I've always loved the hills in the rain. *Much* better than pushing one's way past hundreds of people with umbrellas!"

"It is, of course, but I just didn't realize. Even the mud isn't bad. After the first five minutes you give up caring. Gwenfron——"

"Yes?"

"How are you going to bear being indoors all the time? Struggling with bed pans and blanket baths and trying patients? I should think you'd burst with frustration."

Over Gwenfron's face came a particularly thoughtful expression.

"I can't explain; indeed I can't, Catrin. I shall miss the hills, but I shan't really *mind*. They'll still be here when I come home. I'm longing for September and the begining of my new life."

I gave her a wondering look and went on my way alone, marveling at the difference in people. I had seen quite a bit of one hospital, at least during the past few weeks, and though I admired the nurses with all my heart, I was always glad to get away from the long wards full of sufferers and the bleak, bare corridors. To make it one's life, willingly and even eagerly, was beyond me. But perhaps I would learn to understand as I got to know Gwenfron better.

I liked the hills in the rain and I liked our own valley, too. There were a lot of flowers by then and I was learning the names—ragged robin and campion, early purple and common spotted orchids, and many others. I think that until then I had imagined the countryside filled with a strictly limited number of wild flowers, mainly buttercups and daisies, bluebells and wild roses.

Once when I wailed to Gwenfron that I should never learn all the names, she replied cheerfully:

"Wait until later! June and July. That little wood between the village and the Priory is simply filled with bellflowers and dozens of other flowers."

"Well, teach me all you can," I said, and went to pick marsh marigolds on the wet ground by the stream to brighten my dark rooms at the Priory.

In the bad weather there were few visitors, but I was too busy to find life dull. I was quite happy during the day, but I looked forward to the evenings. The choir practices, for instance. I was very shy and nervous at the first one, and I certainly wondered how Millicent would have felt surrounded by so many Welsh-speaking people, but everyone was very kind to me, and Mr. Evans seemed to find my voice up to standard. In fact, when he had listened to me sing "All Through the Night" in Welsh, he looked quite moved and said:

"Indeed a beautiful voice! And for an English girl to sing in Welsh——"

"My mother was Welsh," I told him.

"And she taught you to sing our lovely songs? Lucky you were, indeed. And now you shall sing at the International Eisteddfod. Get the first prize we will one day!"

The village hall was very small and rather depressing, but I soon forgot to notice. Everyone worked so hard, and I had to work especially hard, not letting my mind wander, because of the difficulty of understanding so little Welsh. All the same, my eyes did travel sometimes to the faces about me. Mr. Jones from the inn, singing away as though his life depended on it . . . Gwenfron, so pretty and so much in earnest, usually beside me . . . Ifor, who seemed to take the local choir as seriously as he took the sale of film rights.

After the first choir practice Gwenfron walked home with me, but after the second she was kept back by Mrs. Griffith and I found Ifor by my side.

"I'll see you back to the Priory," he said briefly, and then added, "If you'd like me to?"

"Yes, thank you," I said, a little surprised, for it was still broad daylight, though misty on account of the steadily falling rain. It was pleasant to walk with Ifor through the soft, dim evening, but I didn't really understand the happiness that filled me. It didn't even abate much when we passed the inn and I saw Olwen staring out at us. Olwen wasn't in the choir, having, as Gwenfron said with rather unusual lack of charity, a terrible voice.

"It's a lonely spot," Ifor remarked as we lingered by the Priory gates for a moment.

I wondered whether to tell him about the blue light and the moans, but it was, after all, several nights earlier, and there had been no recurrence. And I didn't want him to think me silly and nervous when we were just beginning to get almost friendly.

So I said nothing and he went away, and a couple of

hours later, when I was just ready for bed, there was the most resounding knock on the front door.

My heart leaped when I remembered that the outer gates were bolted and no one could get in. But someone *had* got in, and the knocking was urgent and unnerving. Dai was barking wildly, and the moment I opened the kitchen door he bounded off along the passage. But I had to find my flashlight and go much more carefully. I had taught myself to respect the unexpected steps, corners, and arches, for I had no wish to have an accident and lie there until discovered.

The knocking had stopped, and Dai was snuffling against the foot of the door, not looking particularly upset, just curious.

"Who's there?" I shouted, but there was no answer. No sound at all anywhere.

Uneasily I turned and went into the big sitting room and made my way through the massive old furniture to the window, which looked out onto the cloister garth and also to the steps by the front door.

It was by then quite dark, and I could see almost nothing, but there seemed to be no one on the steps.

In the end I went back to the door and unbolted it, flashing my light out into the rainy darkness. Nothing at all! And Dai merely stood by my side, sniffing the air and obviously unwilling to get himself wet.

As I locked the door again I realized that my legs were shaking and my hands cold. It was so very *queer*.

I was so bothered that I made myself a cup of tea and stood by the dying fire while I drank it. I told myself that on no account must I get rattled. There was, there must be, some perfectly reasonable explanation of the moaning, blue lights, and resounding knocks on the door.

The next morning, which was dry, I made a complete circuit of the Priory walls on the outside. There was no back entrance to the house, and the kitchen window, rather a high one, was the only outlook on that side, apart from Aunt Mair's bedroom. The rest of the ruins were completely walled, and, as I have said, the walls were mostly very high, smooth, and unclimbable. The gates were high, too, with iron spikes on the top. It would certainly take an agile person to invade the ruins, and yet someone must have done so.

So I told myself in broad daylight, but with the fall of darkness I found myself growing a little nervous, and I seriously wondered whether to ask Gwenfron to come down and sleep with me for a few nights. But I was not really bothered enough for that, and I didn't want to make a fuss about something that sounded so unlikely. The same pride that had kept me at the Priory during the first days and nights came to my aid again.

I told myself that I had a dog and that no one could get into the house anyway, and then did my best to forget the mysterious business. But when I went out to Gwyncefn or Llanbryn Farms I left Dai out, so that when I unlocked the gates on my return he would immediately come bounding to meet me.

It was the first week of June, and the nights, in spite of the wet and rather chilly weather, were light until very late. I rarely left Gwyncefn Farm before half past nine or ten, and it was barely beginning to grow dusk by the time I returned home.

Apart from the little mystery, which I refused to let prey on my mind, I was really very happy. Most people in the valley seemed to have accepted me, especially since I joined the choir, and after my lessons and conversations with Gwenfron, my Welsh was improving. I suppose I started with a decided advantage in being familiar with the sound of the language and in knowing the words of some songs. At any rate, I was a quick pupil, and Gwenfron seemed astonished. I myself was surprised to find that I no longer felt quite so shut out when everyone chatted together in the bus.

Yes, everyone seemed to accept and like me except Mrs. Jones and Olwen. Mrs. Jones was never actually unfriendly, but she sometimes had a look in her eyes that I did not care for, and she often asked me when I was leaving the valley.

"Fery lonely you must be, a young girl like you. It issn't right!"

"Oh, I'm used to it now," I said lightly more than once, and I thought to myself that she seemed very eager to get rid of me. Because of her daughter, I supposed; and certainly she much disliked my going up to Gwyncefn Farm.

"Up there plenty, you are!" she said when I collected my meat one morning.

I almost came to the point of telling her to mind her own business, but I couldn't really quarrel with her. For one thing, she was good about ordering things that I needed; and for another, I liked her husband so much.

It must be galling for her, of course, when Olwen was never invited to the farm, but that wasn't my fault. And, as a matter of fact, I was beginning to admit to myself that much of my happiness was rooted in my evenings at Gwyncefn.

I loved the old, beautiful house and was beginning to feel at home there. The old servant who did most of the cooking and cleaning, Megan, seemed to have accepted me as one of the family, and Mrs. Williams quite obviously welcomed my company and was always delighted to talk about music, the theater, and London. She also seemed to like it when Gwenfron and I sang to the harp. I was rather shy of her at first, for she seemed a formidable woman, but I soon learned to admire and like her. She had lost her husband, and all her sons but one were away in Canada, but she was always busy and interested and she never complained.

"Mother would like to go to Canada for a long visit or perhaps to live," Gwenfron told me one day. "But she doesn't like to leave Ifor. Of course, if he married it would be different, but he doesn't take much interest in girls. By the way, I'm very glad that you get on with him well now."

It was true. I did get on quite well with Ifor Williams. Our better understanding began, I think, that day in Llangollen when he gave me my "welcome to Wales," and it increased a week or so later when we had all been watching a television play and started discussing it afterward.

At last I found myself talking to him with reasonable intelligence, and when he and Gwenfron walked home with me we were still arguing and discussing animatedly. It was stimulating to meet a mind that was well educated, questioning, and imaginative, and Gwenfron, too, did not fall far behind. It began to seem as though I had found, in a lonely Welsh valley, two of the most interesting possible companions.

What with housework, shopping, dealing with visitors, and going to see Aunt Mair, I did not have a great deal of free time during the day, but when the weather improved in early June I sometimes helped up at the farm. The first hay was already cut, and its fragrance filled the whole valley. Gwenfron rode about on the hayrake, looking completely happy and sometimes singing at the top of her voice, and Ifor, I, and the men gathered the hay into little heaps. It was harder work than I had supposed, but it was lovely to be out in the sun, and I always enjoyed the moments of relaxation in the hedge, when we drank tea and ate sandwiches. Sometimes I lay on my back and looked up at a frieze of wild roses against the hills and the very blue sky. But it was never for long, for there was always more hay to cock or turn, or else the poultry to feed and the eggs to collect.

One never-to-be-forgotten day I actually drove the cows up to the farmyard, marching along like a real farmer's boy with a stick in my hand.

And Ifor, meeting the herd and me at the gate, grinned and said:

"Well, now, Catrin! And isn't this a sight that gladdens my heart!"

"So long as you keep the bull out of my way," I retorted, thinking that his old farm clothes really suited him better than town ones. In his blue shirt and breeches and boots, with his sun-tanned limbs and crisp dark hair, he looked astonishingly handsome.

"I will, though he's really quite harmless. Now why not go the whole way and come and learn how to milk?"

I hesitated, looking at him as the last of the herd passed peacefully into its appointed stall and began to munch cattle cake, and he laughed, putting a warm hand on my arm for a moment.

"Come along. I won't let any harm come to you."

It was very quiet and peaceful in the cowshed. Through the open windows came the distant rattle of the hayrake and the shouts of the men, but we seemed very much alone. The cows munched and swished their tails, and sparrows twittered about the open door.

To my astonishment the milk came easily, and there was a certain pleasure in falling into a steady rhythm.

"Why! It's easy!" I gasped, and Ifor laughed.

"Not for everyone. Some people are very clumsy and awkward and don't get anything. You've just got the knack; sensitive fingers, partly. Just keep on with her. She's very quiet."

So I sat there almost placidly, with one arm against the cow's warm flank, and the milk splashed steadily into the pail. Behind me Ifor began to milk, too, and I found myself trying to match his rhythm, so that the milk flowed faster.

Gwenfron, finding me there twenty minutes later, stared in amazement.

"Oh, Catrin! And you said you were afraid."

"I was," I said. "But not any more. This is my third cow, and it *is* easy. But oh! my poor wrists!"

"They'll be stiff tomorrow," Ifor remarked, carrying some of the milk away to the dairy to be cooled and measured. "You've done very well, Catrin."

And when I returned to the Priory I found myself looking back at that short time alone with Ifor, with the sunlight slanting in and the smell of straw and cattle food, as oddly idyllic. I wondered what on earth Penelope would have said if she had seen me. But Penelope was far away in Paris, reveling in her contacts with a new country. Always a sophisticated girl, I was sure that she would not understand my new happiness. I did not wholly understand it myself.

So June passed rapidly, and sometimes it seemed to me as though I had always lived in Nant Gwyncefn. Each day made me more at home in the valley.

In the town, and in every cottage and farm in the neighborhood, no doubt, there was endless talk of the coming Eisteddfod. I had been to see the field in Llangollen where the vast marquee would go up, and all the bookable seats had been sold long ago for the whole week.

The Williamses had several tickets for each day and for the evening concerts, and Mrs. Williams said I could go whenever I liked. I was particularly looking forward to what sounded the most exciting session: the one when the foreign groups danced. Teams were expected from Spain, Yugoslavia, Scotland, Germany, Austria, Italy, Brittany, and many other countries. The town would be a whirling mass of color once they had arrived in their brilliant national costumes.

"And I might have been back in London!" I said to Gwenfron. "Oh, if only the weather's fine! But I'm scared stiff about the choir. I think I shall be ill on Thursday!"

"Don't you dare!" Gwenfron retorted. "I shall come and fetch you myself. We need every voice we can find, and yours is a lovely one."

"So is yours," I said soberly, for she could still move me, in the beauty of a June evening, when she sat at the harp and played the old, nostalgic airs of her own country.

"Wales!" I would think then, and know that I loved it and wanted to belong. And then I would remember that to Millicent, and perhaps to many other people, that would seem sentimental and absurd. But my Welsh blood was very much alive.

When I went to see Aunt Mair she always exclaimed over how well I looked, and she seemed very glad to know that I was enjoying myself. She herself was much better and was getting around a little, though her leg was being a long business. There seemed little chance that she would be back at the Priory much before the end of July.

Sometimes I forced myself to look toward the future, but it was no use. It almost seemed as though the glorious week of the International Eisteddfod blocked anything that might follow.

With so much to think about, my little mystery had fallen very much into the background, since there had been no manifestation of it for some time. Then, one evening when I was going to bed, it happened again—a thunderous knock at the door.

It was very late, for I had been to the farm and then had sat reading in the kitchen. Darkness had almost fallen.

Once again there was no answer when I called, and once again, when I opened the door, there was neither sight nor sound of a living soul.

More mystery

I stood on the steps, staring into the gloom, and suddenly, from the church, came the sound of a bloodcurdling moan.

It was exceedingly eerie, and yet I did my best not to be frightened. I believed with all my father's English common sense that there was some normal, human explanation. Perhaps the Celtic part of me was not so sure, but I wasn't going to let it get the upper hand.

I locked the front door on the outside and, with the heavy key weighting down my pocket, called Dai and shone my flashlight ahead of me. It was a very strong light that I had bought in Llangollen only a week or two before.

I had left a hoe against the shed earlier in the day and, brandishing it to give myself courage, I crossed the garth and passed between the pillars of the nearest aisle of the church. Dai had bounded ahead with a loud "Wuff!" and had disappeared into the north transept, and I marched after him, swinging flash and hoe, grimly determined to solve the mystery.

But the north transept was quite empty, and there was no way out of it other than the way I had come. It was the south transept that held the dark little opening that led to the sacristy and then to the chapter house.

No way out but the window, which was high, and Dai was standing under it, wagging his tail and grinning up into the light of my flash.

"Well, you don't seem to be worried!" I said rather irritably, flashing the light onto the stones below the window. They would, perhaps, offer a few foot- and hand-holds to an agile person, but on the other side, as I had already noted, the ground dropped several feet and the wall was smooth.

Everywhere was intensely silent, and when I retreated past the site of the high altar the great church loomed above me, the arches faintly marked against the stars.

Dai followed me, gamboling cheerfully, and I felt thoroughly exasperated with him. Was he, or was he not, supposed to be a good house dog? The only possible explanation seemed to be that if someone was trying to frighten me, it was someone known, and not in the least feared, by Dai. But who would do such a thing? It seemed fantastic. Olwen disliked me, but she was certainly not likely to play ghosts, even if she had been able to climb into the ruins. Remembering her tight skirts and rather languid air, I definitely dismissed the idea.

I also dismissed most firmly any lingering doubts about

ghosts in the Priory. It seemed that someone was trying
to frighten me so that I would go away, and I was not
going to be frightened or driven from the Priory. But just
the same, I thoroughly disliked the thought of anyone being able to get into the ruins at will. I was guardian of
Gwyncefn Priory, and I was greatly afraid of damage, apart
from anything else.

Once again, in the bright light of morning, I circled my
domain, both inside and out, and could find nothing,
except that the grass a few feet from the wall under the
transept window looked rather trampled, and there were
one or two small marks, as though something, possibly a
ladder, had rested there. But they could equally well have
been made by the hoofs of cattle in the wet weather.
There were sometimes cows in the field, and, in fact, there
were some at that very moment, away on the far side by
the gate.

It crossed my mind that I might tell my tale to the
police, but there was no policeman in the valley. There
had been once, so I had learned, but there had been so
little need for his presence that, when he retired, no
one was sent to replace him. It would mean going to
Llangollen and, after all, I had so little to tell. A blue
light once, thunderous knocks and moans. Nothing con-
crete at all. They would probably be polite, and they
might send someone to investigate, but they would think,
in their hearts, that it was simply nervousness and too
much imagination on the part of the Priory's solitary ten-
ant. The people in the valley might think the same. They
had always been surprised that I had settled down at the

Priory; some of them thought, or professed to think, that it was an eerie place. They wouldn't blame me, but they might laugh among themselves.

I didn't want to make an idiot of myself. I didn't like the mystery, but if it got no worse it was really preferable to the other course of action. Though I did think I might tell Gwenfron; perhaps I was silly not to have done so before.

I didn't see Gwenfron that day, but the next evening I was expected at the farm. I had a busy time almost until the last minute, for I was clearing out one of the over-crowded bedrooms. There were mountains of rubbish, and I decided that Aunt Mair wouldn't mind if I got rid of some of it. After the Eisteddfod there was to be a jumble sale in the village, and things were already piled up in one of the sheds behind the inn. Mrs. Jones would welcome anything; she had already said so. So I made quite a heap outside the front door, at the edge of the cloister garth, and covered the whole with an old mackintosh sheet in case of rain. I planned to ask if the Jones boys could collect it the next day.

After my labors the room looked much better and would easily take the two camp beds. I was dusty and tired but quite pleased with myself as I washed and changed and set off for Gwyncefn.

Ifor had been to London for the night to sign his film contract, but he was back when I arrived and full of plans about what he was going to do with the money. Part of the house would be redecorated, a new cowshed built, and various new farm implements bought. He was in a very animated mood, and after supper I walked around the farm with him, since Gwenfron was making herself a new dress and was struggling with one of the sleeves.

"But I shan't start anything until after the Eisteddfod," Ifor said as we leaned on the garden wall, looking down into the valley. "The house will be full of Italians for nearly a week. After that——" And he looked around lovingly.

"You—you do like it all?" I ventured. I was not really shy of him any more; in fact, we seemed to gravitate together when we could. But I didn't feel that I was anywhere near to understanding his complex nature.

He ran his brown hand along the smooth stones of the wall, still warm from the day's sun.

"Yes. I wouldn't leave here—no, indeed, not for anything. But if this success is going on I may employ a man to manage the farm when I'm away. There's that good little house on the far side of the buildings. It's been empty for some time, but it's dry and has electric light and plumbing. I've heard of a man who might be suitable; he's working near Corwen just now. I shall always be here a great deal, but I may want to feel I can stay in London when necessary."

"Were you sorry when your brothers decided to emigrate?"

He shrugged.

"They had no wish to stay, and they're doing well in Canada. It meant that I got the farm, and I must admit I was glad of that. I'm a Welshman and I want to stay in my own country."

In the end it was very late when I was ready to leave the farm. We got talking after supper, and then there was a television performance of the ballet *Casse Noisette* that I wanted to see. It was getting dark as I put on my red jacket, and Gwenfron and Ifor both said that they would accompany me.

"I'm not afraid," I said. "I really don't mind the country in the dark now."

"All the same," said Ifor firmly, "we'll go with you. The lane's very rough, and you might sprain an ankle and have to stay there till morning."

"It's not a bit likely," I said, but I was glad of their company. It was pleasant to stroll through the warm night with two people I liked so much, and perhaps the darkness was a help, for I found myself, as we approached the Priory, telling them about my mystery. Rather to my surprise, they both listened perfectly seriously, and Ifor seemed disturbed.

"But it's extraordinary! Who would do such a thing?" Gwenfron cried. "Why on earth didn't you tell us before, Catrin? We'll have to get to the bottom of it."

"I wish we could," I said. "But there's really been so very little, and the happenings have been quite far apart. I thought you'd laugh."

"Laugh!" Ifor repeated rather grimly. "And what would you be thinking of us if we laughed? Cows are one thing, Catrin Drury, but mysterious knocks and blue lights quite another. It sounds as though someone wants to frighten you badly."

"But who?" I asked helplessly. "And it's so hard to get into the ruins."

Gwenfron said firmly:

"Catrin, I suppose I can't come tonight, as it's so late

and I haven't got any of my things, but I'll sleep with you for a few nights, starting tomorrow. We'll watch and set traps, and perhaps——"

"And nothing will happen," I retorted. "After all, the first time was weeks ago, and——"

"All the same, I'm coming. Don't you think I ought to, Ifor?"

Ifor was silent for a moment, then he said:

"I do indeed. I don't like the sound of it, though it doesn't seem as though anyone means you serious harm. Just to frighten you—and you haven't been frightened."

"Very brave you are," said Gwenfron. "I always thought so, and now——" She sniffed. "What a strong smell of burning!"

"So there is!" I agreed, suddenly realizing that I had been half conscious of it for some minutes. It came from the Priory, too.

We had come by the lane that crossed the little river close under the crags and were already passing behind the house and approaching the gates. Dai started to bark, perhaps hearing our approach, or perhaps upset by that rapidly increasing smell. There was smoke now, acrid and alarming.

"I put the kitchen fire out," I cried, fumbling with the key that opened the padlock. The gates swung back, Dai darted out, capering and barking frantically, and I half expected to see the house flaming before my eyes. But it was dark and apparently quite safe, and the smell came from our right.

"It's from the chapter house!" Gwenfron shouted, but Ifor and I had already realized it, too. We went dashing toward the doorway as a wave of thick smoke poured out. Inside the chapter house it was very dark, but there was a red glow in a corner. As we approached, long flames licked out.

Horribly frightened, and coughing painfully, I turned on my flash and saw that a great heap of rubbish had been piled against the wall under the rose window. It was already quite red at the heart, and each second the flames and smoke increased.

My one thought was for the building—for its beautiful gray walls and the perpendicular vaulting that remained in that corner.

"I'll get a rake or something!" I shouted and turned and dashed across the garth toward the shed, followed by my companions.

"Water?" Ifor demanded, and I gasped:

"There's a tap in the corner past the front door, and a bucket by it. Only don't fall over the things I left piled up for the jumble sale."

Gwenfron and I flew back with implements, and I heard Ifor running the tap. The fire was burning so fiercely that the chapter house was filled with a flickering glow, so that, even in the smoke, the vaulting showed clearly. Then there was a thicker wave of smoke and I coughed and choked.

The heat was considerable, but I raked madly, leaping away from the burning fragments that fell about my feet. On the other side Gwenfron was doing the same, and Ifor suddenly shouted:

"Stand back for a moment!"

The water hurtled, hissing, over the fire and poured

down the stones, and we all coughed as the smoke and steam increased. Ifor handed the bucket to Gwenfron, seizing her rake, and we worked frantically to scatter the fire and stamp and beat it out. I couldn't hold my flash and wield my rake, and it was like working blind. My eyes were streaming, in any case, and my throat felt like sandpaper.

Gwenfron returned and the water hissed on the fire. Ifor cried triumphantly:

"That's done it, I think! It hadn't really taken hold thoroughly. But we'd better make sure."

Two minutes later we staggered out into the blessed fresh air on the garth. There was still some smoke and a frightful smell of burning, but the danger was past. While Gwenfron and I strove to get our breath, Ifor poured one more bucket of water over the charred mess in the chapter house. Then his dark figure joined us. The stars were growing bright, and it was just light enough for us to be able to see a little.

Dai, wildly excited and upset, milled around our feet.

"It was frightful!" I gasped, mopping my eyes. "How *could* it have happened? It was my rubbish! I recognized one of the boxes and a moth-eaten old tablecloth. But I really did leave it over by the front door to be collected tomorrow for the jumble sale." My legs were shaking, and I felt shamefully near to tears. "I wouldn't have had it happen—— The Priory——"

Ifor's hand was on my arm, and it was strangely comforting.

"A good thing that we were with you and no real damage done. Are you all right, Gwenfron?"

"Dry as a ditch in summer, but all right otherwise!" said Gwenfron.

"Come in and have something to drink," I said shakily, and I fetched the door key from the hiding place that I chose afresh almost every time I went out.

We all went into the kitchen, and Ifor lit the lamp and the oil stove while Gwenfron and I washed our blackened hands and drank some cold water. While the kettle boiled we stared at one another. Our clothes were blackened and singed and our faces smoke-grimed. Gwenfron had a burn on her leg, and I one on my wrist, but they weren't very bad and were soon soothed by some stuff I found in Aunt Mair's little medicine chest.

"Don't *worry,* Catrin," Gwenfron begged. "It's all right. The chapter house won't really be harmed, though it will look terrible in the morning."

"But it was deliberate," I said, still trying hard not to cry with reaction and shock. "All that stuff—— Someone carried it into the chapter house and deliberately set fire to it. Someone wicked or—or simple. You do hear of people setting fire to things because—because——"

Ifor was sitting on the edge of the table, absent-mindedly smoothing his hair.

"I don't like it any better than you do. It was, as you say, deliberate wickedness. Another thing to frighten you, but going much farther than blue lights and knocks. Whoever did it may have thought you were at home and in bed. Perhaps they meant to knock when the fire was really burning. But we took them by surprise——"

"There wasn't anyone——" I said weakly, thankful to see that the kettle was just on the point of boiling.

"There must have been. They'd have had warning when they heard us approaching and you unlocking the padlock. It was pretty dark, and whoever it was could have slipped out through the sacristy and into the nave."

I made the tea, trying to stop my hands from shaking, and we drank three cups each, not speaking much. Then Ifor said, in a voice that can only be described as masterful:

"Catrin, you can't stay here. I don't for a moment think that anyone means you any harm. I think it's someone who has a grudge against you and wants to frighten you away, for some unknown reason. But you must come home with us, indeed you must."

I stared at him and found that my trembling had quite stopped.

"It's nice of you, but I can't come. I'm in charge here, and I must stay. If we hadn't found the fire in time——"

"But, Catrin——"

Gwenfron interrupted quietly:

"She means it, Ifor, so I'll stay with her. She can lend me pajamas and anything else I need. And you'll have to tell Mother why, I'm afraid, but try not to alarm her."

Ifor looked at me almost with exasperation. He seemed very big in the lamplight, though he was not actually so very many inches taller than I.

"Bravery is all very well, but there's no point in it. Nothing more will happen tonight——"

"Then we can stay!" I said triumphantly. "I'm not leaving here, anyway, but I'll be very glad of Gwenfron's company. This is my Priory for the time being——"

"They don't pay you to be frightened out of your wits,"

Ifor retorted, so sharply that Gwenfron looked quite
startled. "Still, have it your own way. I'll be getting back,
or Mother will be really worried. And tomorrow I shall
go to the police."

"Oh, but——" I protested weakly, impressed, in spite
of myself, by his show of anger.

"No buts. They'll have to know, though I much doubt
if they can do anything. Get to bed as quickly as you can."

We followed him out onto the garth, and I held the
gates for a moment, looking after him. He turned after a
few steps and said more quietly:

"Good night, Catrin."

"Good night, Ifor," I said meekly, and then Gwenfron
and I retreated into the house and washed and undressed
in the kitchen. She said she didn't mind sharing the big
bed with me, and we were soon tucked in comfortably,
half asleep when our heads touched the pillows.

In the morning it was raining, which somehow did not
improve the appearance of the chapter house. Owing to
our prompt action, the walls were only a little blackened,
but the broken stone floor was littered with the most in-
describable mess. By the time we had cleared it away
we were hot and tired, and there was not a great deal we
could do to improve the appearance of the floor. In time
the marks of burning would disappear and the grass grow
green again where it came up in patches between the
flags, but just then the sight was rather a sorry one.

I looked gloomily at the pile of half-burned rubbish in
the wheelbarrow.

"What do we do with this?"

Just then the police arrived, in the shape of Sergeant Jones frm Llangollen. Ifor had, of course, already told the story, but we had to tell it again, and he examined the chapter house and the rubbish without, apparently, coming to any other conclusion than that it was malicious damage. He asked several times if I had any enemies in the valley, or if Aunt Mair had, and I answered that, so far as I knew, there was no one. I could hardly accuse Mrs. Jones or Olwen of doing such a fantastic thing, and there was no one else.

He went off in the end, saying that he must ask some questions in the village. Perhaps someone had seen a suspicious character—maybe a tramp—the previous evening. He seemed to think very little of blue lights, moans, and knocks. As I had feared, he looked all too ready to dismiss those as the wild imaginings of a young girl living alone in a strange, lonely place.

I felt indignant when he had gone, and, as Gwenfron and I set to work to dig a hole for the rubbish in the soft ground under the trees opposite the gates, my thoughts went round and round.

"I'll solve it somehow!" I said fiercely as I jammed down the frightful old tablecloth and began to push back the earth. "I must solve it before those Swiss people arrive. I'm not going to have things spoiled for them."

Ifor came down at lunchtime to see how we were getting on, and seemed much relieved to find the chapter house no worse.

"Indeed, it's a wretched business, but perhaps nothing

more will happen. Maybe the culprit will be scared by all the fuss. I've thought and thought, but there's no apparent explanation."

There did, indeed, seem no way of explaining things. The fire at the Priory and the suggestion of other mysterious happenings were sources of wonder all over the valley, and most people came to look at the chapter house and to shake their heads in a puzzled way. Even Mrs. Jones came, wearing her best hat and coat, though I was ready to bet that she had never shown the slightest interest in the chapter house before. She shook her head very worriedly and then looked long at me.

"You'll not be staying here, girl? Not after such a fery bad fright! A tramp it must have been, but still—— Always a strange place, this old Priory!"

Well, I could not suspect her of having anything to do with the business, but there was no doubt that she was relishing my imminent departure. I hastened to alter her ideas.

"No, I shall not be going. If there's any more trouble I mean to get to the bottom of it. Gwenfron's going to sleep here with me for a few nights, and we'll keep a careful watch."

"Well, I nefer!" she cried, shaking her head until her best hat rose on her carefully waved hair. She paid nearly as many visits to a hairdresser in Llangollen as her daughter did. "Well, I nefer!"

"I nefer either!" I said to myself when she had gone. "But one thing's certain. Catrin Drury's stayed so long that she's not leaving now."

There was too much to keep me in Nant Gwyncefn.

Catrin in danger

Gwenfron stayed with me for several nights, but nothing more happened at all. We patrolled the ruins every night before going to bed, and we set minor traps in the way of pieces of string tied from one pillar to another, but the string was never broken nor was there the slightest sign that anyone had invaded our domain.

In a few days the mystery at the Priory was almost forgotten in the greater excitement of the coming Eisteddfod. No one could talk of anything else. The town, the cottages, the farms buzzed with it.

The marquee and all the smaller tents were up, and Gwenfron and I went to the Eisteddfod ground to see all there was to be seen, which was not much. But there was something immensely impressive about standing in that vast, empty marquee, built to hold many thousands of people. There was also something very terrifying in the thought of standing on that stage, in front of the huge audience. And yet soloists did it, and even small boys and girls, whereas I would at least be in the company of other singers.

We stood at the very back, with the rows of seats stretching away and away, and Gwenfron said:

"Oh, Catrin! Wait till you see the flowers. Very lovely they always are round the stage. And then on the Tuesday night———"

Tuesday night would see the opening of the Eisteddfod. The first concert would be a wonderful experience, and our seats were in the fourth row. There was to be a foreign ballet company and a great orchestra. Then the next day the folk dancing—how I was looking forward to it! Especially the two Spanish teams. I had seen Spanish dancing in London and had found myself quite carried away by its life and color and the wild flamenco singing.

"My Swiss come on Monday evening," I said. "They're traveling right through, so they'll be dead tired. Oh, Gwenfron! Isn't it exciting?"

"And ours from Milan come Tuesday afternoon," Gwenfron told me. "They're members of a great choir."

It was certainly very thrilling. The decorations and flags were going up in the town, and all plans seemed well in hand. The organization of the great Eisteddfod seemed to me a miracle of efficiency. Every soul in the neighborhood really cared that it should be a success. The world was coming to the Dee Valley and to all the other little valleys and remote villages, and it should be well received.

The only unfortunate thing was the weather, which had turned very gray and chilly, but we hoped passionately that it would have time to change. We wanted the dancers to be able to dance in the streets, drift in boats and barges along the canal, and sit on the rocks by the river in their brilliant national costumes, as they had done in other years. I had never seen them, of course, but I had heard plenty about it, and Gwenfron had many photographs.

The beds at the Priory were ready, and I had placed a huge grocery order. But, though I was both busy and excited, I had never quite forgotten the "mystery" and my determination to solve it. I did tend to look at almost everyone from the valley with a faint trace of suspicion, wondering if there were one among them who would be likely to play unpleasant tricks. But it seemed more fantastic than ever. Nearly all of them seemed nice, sober people who liked and more or less accepted me. I saw little of Olwen; occasionally we passed each other in the lane, or she was about when I called at the inn; that was all. We always smiled at each other rather warily, she, at least, in no very friendly way, but I could not seriously suspect her.

As time passed and the Eisteddfod was almost upon us I decided that nothing more mysterious would happen and that whoever had been responsible had been frightened by the fuss caused by the blaze in the chapter house.

On the Sunday before the Eisteddfod I went to Wrexham to see Aunt Mair, who was just on the point of leaving for a convalescent home. We had got to know each other quite well during my visits to the hospital and I had grown fond of her, and she, I think, of me.

She smiled at me very warmly as she sat in one of the big chairs at the end of the ward.

"It's been a long time, Catrin, indeed it has. I never thought that I should be in the hospital for eight weeks. Good it will be to be back in the country and to feel the sun." Then she put out a thin hand. "You've been a very good, faithful girl! Indeed, I couldn't have wished for a better niece."

"Oh, nonsense!" I cried, rather embarrassed. "I haven't done much. Actually, I've liked it. I didn't at first, but mostly I've enjoyed it. You'll find Dai and the cats—and the Priory, of course—well looked after when you come back at the end of the month."

"And what about you, my dear?" she asked. "You'll go back to London, I suppose, and find a job in an office?"

"I don't know," I said. "Yes, I suppose so." And when I left her my heart was suddenly heavy. My time in Nant Gwyncefn would soon be over, and I found that I most deeply dreaded the thought of the parting. Never to see the farm again; never to go cycling and walking over the hills with Gwenfron, discussing so many things; never to see Ifor . . .

But I pushed the thoughts away. Once I was back in London I should probably feel differently. I should be busy, finding a job and settling in with Penelope. But Penelope was not yet back from Paris. They had asked her to stay on for a while. If Penelope didn't ever come back . . .

Once again I wrestled with my thoughts, and, leaving the bus near Bishop Trevor's bridge, it was easier to forget them. For the flags were up, blowing gaily in the gray air, and the red dragon of Wales bade visitors a welcome.

That evening the weather forecast was miraculously better, and I went to bed in a hopeful frame of mind. After all, why worry about the future? I had a few weeks left. The Eisteddfod was about to begin, and the sun was going to shine. For the first night in a week there were stars and a cloudy moon.

The sun did shine. I awoke to a blaze of gold, and summer had come back to the valley. The hills were green with the deep July bracken; the whole valley looked bright and warm and most beautiful.

It *was* warm, as I found when I stepped out onto the cloister garth. The old house was always cool, or even dead cold, but the garth was bathed in light and heat. The cats rolled in the sun, delighted and relaxed, and Dai rolled, too, all four feet waving in the air.

I carried my breakfast outside and ate it on one of the stones over by the wall of the chapter house. Then I did what little work there was left, reviewed my stores in the cellarium, and felt that I could not stay indoors. But I supposed that I had better stay somewhere near the Priory, in case the visitors already in the town decided to visit the ruins, so I took a book and wandered over the field to the bank of the river. The little brown stream rushed on its way to the Dee, with a tangle of low trees and bushes on either bank.

I flung down my book and kicked off my sandals and paddled for a time, seeing my brown feet strangely through the clear, moving water. It was rather cold after all the rain, but delightfully refreshing, and I felt on top of the world—bareheaded, bare-limbed, with the sunlit hills all around and the great Priory church looming up across the field.

Then I sat down in a hollow to read, looking up occasionally to glance at the lane, which I could just see through the trees. If anyone came to the Priory I should probably see or hear them; I should certainly hear when they rang the bell by the gate.

But the only sounds I heard were shouts from some of the higher fields of Gwyncefn Farm, where the men and perhaps Ifor were working.

Then suddenly I heard voices quite near at hand and a splashing noise.

The voices were shrill and young, and they were speaking in Welsh.

By then I was able to understand Welsh fairly well. After all, it was spoken in the village all the time and, helped by my radio lessons, I was becoming quite proficient. I recognized the voices almost at once. Idris and Inigo Jones were talking about *me!*

The conversation went something like this:

"Why ever not? We could think of something much better than lights and knocking to scare that Catrin with."

"No, Inigo, never again! You know what Olwen said when she guessed what we'd done? She said we were silly and wicked and if we got into trouble she wouldn't help us. And that policeman—— Oh, he frightened me!"

"But it was such very great fun! Exciting, like the things boys do in comics. It's so dull here, with only the old Eisteddfod."

"But Inigo——"

The pair of them were almost opposite me, paddling

in the middle of the stream, before the full significance of their words dawned on me.

"Come here!" I said sharply, dropping my book and thrusting my feet into my sandals.

Idris gave me one horrified look, his dark little face suffused with color, then he gave a cry, started to move, and slipped on the bed of the stream. For a moment he stayed there, staring at me openmouthed, then he shouted something in Welsh, scrambled to his feet, and tore away after his brother.

"Stop!" I yelled with all the authority of which I was capable. "I want to speak to you!"

But they had gone, tearing along the bank of the stream, brushing past bushes that caught at their shabby shorts. I wasted a few moments fastening my sandals, then I was after them. My blood was up, for now I knew, as perhaps I should have guessed long before, the source of my mystery.

The Jones boys, sly and mischievous, would be up to anything!

I tore after them, disregarding dignity, determined to catch them and wring the full truth from them before they had time to think up any excuses. And they'd be lucky if they escaped with only a scolding. If I could get my hands on them . . .

They had reached the bridge now and were hesitating. If they turned around past the Priory my longer legs could probably overtake them, and if they turned uphill toward Gwyncefn Farm . . . But they did neither. They went on, pelting over the stony ground almost under the limestone cliff. Their feet were bare, and more than once they gave agonized yelps as the sharp stones caught them. But they scarcely looked behind; they seemed consumed with panic.

"Stop!" I ordered, pretty breathless after the unexpected chase.

Then Idris suddenly twisted around, doubled past me, and was away. But my attention was on Inigo. I suddenly knew what he was going to do.

"Inigo, stop at once! I only want to talk to you. You can't climb up there."

But Inigo could and would. He was already ten feet up the cliff and scrabbling wildly for more foot- and hand-holds. Where he was climbing the way was not difficult, but he could surely never hope to get up to the top? It was almost the highest part. Farther to the left would have been much more possible . . .

My blouse was sticking to my back, and I pushed my hair from my hot forehead. Suddenly I was frightened.

Inigo glanced back over his shoulder, and his eyes looked odd. I wondered if, in one of those strange fantasies of childhood, he was imagining himself really in danger, really chased by an enemy.

He climbed on almost at once, kicking and scrambling, using fingers and toes and bare knees where the ledges were wide enough.

I watched helplessly, glad that at least the cliff itself threw a patch of deep shadow. Up and up the child went, and now it looked to me as though, three quarters of the way up, he could go no farther. He had reached a narrow ledge where one or two small bushes and little waterfalls of harebells and scabiosa grew out of the solid rock.

When I turned I found that Idris had crept back and was standing, small and frightened, fifty yards away.

"Tell him to come down," I said. "I shan't harm him, silly child. I only wanted to talk to you both."

"He issn't able to come down," the older boy said on a slightly wobbly note. "I think he's stuck."

It was all too true. Inigo was clinging to the ledge, looking very small and helpless at that height, and above him there was a decided overhang.

"If you can't get up, Inigo, you'll have to climb down again," I called, trying to keep my voice calm.

He called something breathlessly in Welsh, and I translated it as:

"I can't move! I'm scared!"

I was scared, too. Suddenly the sunlit valley was oddly menacing and most deathly silent.

"Stay still and you'll be all right!" Then I turned to Idris. "Go and tell someone what's happened and ask them to bring a rope. Gwyncefn Farm's nearest. There may be someone in one of the fields. I heard them just now."

He stared at me like a half-wit, his face sharper than usual.

"Our Inigo iss going to die!"

"He certainly will if you don't hurry! Run as fast as you can and shout for help!"

Suddenly he came to life and flew off, yelling at the top of his voice, and I came to a decision. Perhaps it was a silly one, but I couldn't leave that child clinging there in such terror. Obviously he had lost his nerve, but if some-one was near him perhaps he could be persuaded to climb down backwards very slowly. Upwards, I was quite certain, was hopeless, though it would have been reasonably easy farther to the left for anyone with a good head for heights.

I had sometimes climbed on cliffs during seaside holidays, and my sandals had ridged crepe soles that might give a good grip if only the rock were dry. But I had no great hope that it would be after so much rain, especially when the cliff was mostly in heavy shadow. I called:

"It's all right, Inigo! Just stay there. I'm coming up to help."

The first twenty feet or so were easy, but after that it was much more difficult. However, with longer arms and legs than Inigo, I made it without too much trouble, though I didn't dare to look down.

"You can't go on," I said quietly as I drew almost level with him. "So you'll have to try and climb down."

He gave a terrified whimper. He was more or less kneeling on the ledge, clutching a little bush with one hand.

"No, indeed! No, Miss, I can't!"

I clung there, with my nose very close to a patch of yellow stonecrop, not liking the situation at all.

"Inigo, pull yourself together! You must have climbed here before."

"Yess, Miss. But not just here. Fery dangerous it iss here!"

"You might have thought of that before," I said, noting with horror that the bush looked none too strong. A little of the sparse earth came away and trickled past my left ear. My own position was none too good, and, ridiculously, memories of the stories I had liked when I was very young flashed through my mind. Someone always got stuck on a cliff and was rescued by the heroine, but then there had usually been a breaking sea below. Now there was stony ground farther below than I liked to think.

All my senses seemed very alert, and I was sharply conscious of smells and little sounds—something they never told one in the stories. I could smell the hills and the cold rock, and I could hear the soft swishing of the river and of the little waterfalls. Sheep in the far distance, too, and even a faraway tractor.

The child was very near me, and I put my arm behind him by way of comfort, though it could have been no help if he had suddenly lurched off the ledge. I could see the tense muscles through his thin shirt, and his grubby brown hands were tense, too, the right one grasping the stone.

"If you can't climb down," I said quietly, "just stay quite still until someone comes with a rope. They can't be long now."

But it seemed a very long time indeed, and I was by no means sure how long I could hold my position. It seemed better to talk, so I said:

"It will be all right, you know. Soon you'll be having your dinner as though nothing had happened."

He gave a sort of gulp.

"I am not wanting my dinner. I feel sick!"

"You'll stop feeling sick when you get up safely."

Then suddenly he burst out:

"It wass us. You were hearing what we said? We wass

ghosts in the Priory. Climbed out of our bedroom window, we did. Easy it iss, with the old pear tree there. No one wass knowing."

"Why did you do it?" I asked.

He gave another gulp.

"It wass for fun. Fery dull it iss, nothing but old school and playing in the valley."

"But what put the idea into your heads?"

Another gulp and a sniff, and a bit more earth came away from the root of the bush.

"It wass our Olwen. Fery angry she wass because you were going to the farm and walking out with Ifor Williams. Always fancied Ifor Williams, our Olwen hass. Heard our mam say so. Olwen said to Mam she said: 'Indeed I'd give anything for that girl to go away from the Priory. A pity it iss that something doesn't frighten her off. Give five pounds, I would, to see her go!' "

"So you and Idris thought——?"

"Five pounds iss a lot of money," the small, tense child mumbled. "But our Olwen hass plenty of money. Buy us two cowboy outfits that money would, and pictures on Saturdays and comics. So we thought—— I'm going to fall! Indeed I am!"

"No," I said and tightened my arm. The words that had hit me most sharply were "walking out with Ifor Williams." How could Olwen think that? It wasn't true! Ifor and I . . . He had never thought of me like that . . . I had never thought of him. But, clinging there high above the valley, I knew with a sudden sharp pain that I *had*. Only subconsciously, never admitting it even to myself . . .

"But when Olwen found out what you'd been doing——?"

"She wass angry. She said silly we were to bring the
police to the valley. She'd be fery glad to see you go, but
she would nefer pay us five pounds to burn the Priory
down——"

"How did you get into the Priory? Was there a ladder?"

"In the old gatehouse. A barn it iss now. Carried it ofer
the field we did. Only a little one——"

A shout came from somewhere below. I dared not turn
around, even when I recognized Ifor's voice.

"Catrin! Can you hold on? I'll have to get around to the
top." His voice sounded strange and breathless.

"Yes," I called back. "But do be quick!"

I felt that in another few minutes I should lose all sense
of place and time and then I should go hurtling down onto
the stony ground below.

The world comes to Wales

"Will he be pulling me up like a sheep?" asked the small voice against the rock.

"I expect so," I said. "Don't worry. He won't be long now."

But it seemed an hour before I heard sounds above and Ifor's voice called again:

"I'm here, Catrin! And I've got a good strong rope with a noose on the end. Can you get it over Inigo's shoulders and under his arms?"

"I'll try," I said. I felt unlike myself, an odd, floating sensation, and one leg, pressed against the rock wall, had gone to sleep.

"Some more help will be here in a minute. I sent Idris for the men. He met me in the lane, and I dashed for the rope."

The noose dangled gently just above us, and I slowly moved my arm from behind the child and seized it.

"It's going to be—tricky."

"I know. Can't Inigo help himself?"

"Lost his nerve," I explained, but was relieved when Inigo said in a muffled voice:

"I c'n leave go with one hand."

After a minute or two—and it seemed a miracle—the rope was over his head and under one arm. Then, somehow, it was under the other arm and he was obeying Ifor's orders to hold onto the higher part of the rope and use his feet. Up he went, his knees scraping against the rock, and for several breathless moments I half expected him to fall back on me. I didn't dare to look up much, but Ifor's shout told me that he was safe.

"Now you, Catrin. But indeed you must be careful."

There were shouts and running feet somewhere behind me, but I had only thoughts for the dangling rope. I think that those moments of hanging in space, apparently incapable of helping myself, were the worst I had ever known; then I began to use my feet and somehow shot aloft, so that, suddenly, the top of the cliff appeared and I was hauled over onto the thyme-sweet grass. I lay there breathless, my nose against the ground, and when at last I looked up Ifor was sitting not half a yard away, rubbing his wrists. His face was dead white and his eyes very dark.

"Oh, Catrin!" he said. "Come away slowly from that edge."

I moved cautiously and found his arm around me.

"Catrin, when I saw you up there . . . You might have been killed!"

"The child was in more danger," I said, glad of his arm.

I leaned against him, feeling limp and odd. "Where is he?"

"Gone. The little wretch ran off as though nothing had happened. Catrin, my dear . . ." And then he kissed me, so that I thought I must be dreaming or delirious. "Catrin, I love you . . ."

And then the men from the farm came running, having climbed up the easiest way, and we had to calm their anxiety and satisfy their curiosity. I suppose I talked like a normal human being—I know I explained that the boys had been causing trouble at the Priory and had run away from me when I tried to talk to them—but I felt odd and remote as we all made our way down to the valley again.

On the little bridge I know that I said I was perfectly all right, only ravenously hungry, and would go back to the Priory.

"Mrs. Williams wass looking for you," the shepherd said to Ifor. "A telegram there iss."

"Something to do with the Eisteddfod, I expect," said Ifor. "I'll just go back with Catrin. She's too much shaken to be alone."

But I said again that I would be all right and that he'd better go. I wanted desperately to be alone, to sort myself out. And in the end the three men went off, Ifor telling me not to worry and that he would see Mr. Jones about the boys and their behavior at the Priory.

I found myself back in the peace and silence of the ruins, and I went into the house and poured out a huge glass of lemonade. As I sat on the kitchen table to drink it I relived the whole incredible business until I got to that moment on top of the cliff, with the smell of crushed thyme in my nostrils and Ifor's lips on mine.

"Catrin, I love you!"

I *must* have imagined that, even if I had not imagined the kiss—the first real kiss I had ever had. I must have been a little delirious with shock and relief. I must——

I remembered his manner once the men had joined us: quiet and contained, as usual, though he was still rather white.

Of course I had imagined it, or he hadn't meant it. Anyway, I should know when we met again.

But the thought of that meeting filled me with longing and then a sort of terror. If he never referred to it again; if he wished that he had never kissed me . . .

I washed my face and hands and began grimly to prepare my lunch. But my sudden feeling of hunger had gone, and I scarcely noticed what I was eating. Afterwards I washed all over and put on a pretty, cool frock. Visitors might come . . . Ifor might come, though he would be busy at the farm.

Several people did come to the Priory, and I was kept quite busy, which was a good thing, as otherwise I should have been in an even more restless state than I was. At half past five I locked the gates and began to prepare a meal for the eight travelers.

But at six one of the Parry children came with a message from the post office. The Swiss dancers and yodelers would be late; I need not expect them until at least nine o'clock and perhaps even later.

I wondered how on earth I was going to pass the evening and was wandering in the nave when the bell rang again at the outer gate. When I went flying to open the gates there was Gwenfron, her bicycle propped up against the wall.

"Oh!" I cried, and she burst out eagerly:

"Oh, Catrin, I wasn't able to come before. We've been so busy, one way and another. Are you all right? I heard all about that ghastly business this morning. Mother wanted me to come sooner, but Ifor said he thought you were all right, and there really was so much to do. Anyway, we're all ready for the Italians now, and I'm free."

"Yes, of course I'm all right," I said, though my heart had leaped at the mention of Ifor.

"It was a frightful thing to happen."

"My fault, really. I feel very guilty. But I heard those wretched little boys talking by the river, and suddenly I knew it was they who'd done all the frightening things here. I tried to talk to them—I ran after them—and Inigo panicked and climbed the cliff."

"There'll be trouble about the whole business, indeed there will," Gwenfron said. "Ifor said he'd see Mr. Jones on his way to the station. But what he didn't understand was *why* the boys did it."

Of course I hadn't been able to explain that. Even in my dazed state I had known that I couldn't, when it was so much tied up with Olwen's jealousy and dislike. I couldn't even tell Gwenfron properly.

"For adventure, partly, I think," I said. "And then Olwen doesn't like me. They heard her say she'd be glad if I went——"

"I never have liked them," Gwenfron remarked. "Very difficult those boys have been, off and on. We should have thought of them before."

"Was Ifor going to the station to meet someone?" I asked.

"No. He's had a telegram and gone off to London. Something about the casting for his play. They're putting it on sooner than he thought; early in September."

"Oh!" I said, and hoped that I hadn't changed color. "But what about the Eisteddfod—the choir?"

"I've told him that he's got to get back by Wednesday evening at the latest. But the play's all-important just now. We all know that. And Mother and I and Megan can cope with the Italians. You should have seen Megan last year. She could hardly exchange a word with the Swiss people, but she mothered them and bullied them. By the way, I hear *your* Swiss won't be here till late, after all. Let's go into town!"

"Yes, let's!" I cried, in deep relief. It would be something to do, and that was a good deal, when I couldn't hope to see Ifor for two days. Not until Thursday morning, probably. I had little doubt that he would be back in time to sing, but it seemed a lifetime away.

I fetched Aunt Mair's bicycle and we rode away through the golden evening, through the sun splashes under the trees. As we were passing the inn Mrs. Jones signaled to us and we dismounted rather reluctantly. Mrs. Jones looked white and pinched, and her voice was even more shrill than usual.

"It's sorry I am about the boys. Fery wicked they were, and their dad gifing them a hearty good thrashing and sending them to bed in the middle of the day. Stay there till tomorrow and nothing to eat, he said, and lucky the police aren't after them. But still, lads will be lads, and Mr. Williams hadn't any need to be so fery angry——"

"I should think he had every need," Gwenfron said indignantly. "He saw Inigo and Catrin on the cliff. They'd both have been killed, more than likely, but for him. And, in the first place, it was Catrin who saved your boy's life, holding onto him like that. Indeed, you ought to be grateful." I had never seen her look so red-cheeked and angry.

Mrs. Jones' expression was singularly lacking in gratitude as she looked at me.

"They nefer did anything like that when Mrs. Davies wass at the Priory."

Well, I had always known that there were mothers who would defend their children whatever they did, but it seemed a bit thick to blame me, apparently because I had stayed on at the Priory. She *might* perhaps have blamed me for frightening Inigo up the cliff, but that didn't seem to be in her mind at all.

I think I was in rather a strange state, upset and excited and not at all my usual self, and I felt my temper rising. But just in time Mr. Jones appeared and motioned his wife to leave us. This she did with evident reluctance, and the nice little man said gravely:

"A terrible thing indeed, and my own lads! Nefer get ofer it, I won't. Mischievous they've been before—in trouble they've been before, too—but to be frightening such a nice young lady and starting a fire at the Priory . . . So upset I am that I've eaten nothing since Inigo came home, babbling out such a tale. And then Mr. Williams wass coming . . . Oh, indeed, I'm fery sorry!"

He looked so genuinely upset that my temper died.

"It's over and we'd better forget about it," I said. "We're just going into Llangollen to see people arrive."

"Expecting our Swiss people same time as yours," he said. "The Germans have arrived up the valley. They were sitting by the river singing like angels when I wass passing just now."

We rode on and, sure enough, on the banks of the stream near Llanbryn Farm were several men and girls in gay national costumes, and their nostalgic song came over to us, clear in the quiet air. They waved and called *"Gruss Gott!"* and we waved back.

In the town there was a great congestion of traffic, and we left the bikes and pushed our way on foot. The bright evening sunlight lay over the hills and the little gray town, and the flags looked ten times more brilliant than they had done in the dull weather. There were cars and buses and motor coaches, and Eisteddfod organizers, wearing badges, were working desperately to sort it all out, helped by extra police.

A train came in from the Chester direction as we stood on the bridge, and out burst such a kaleidoscope of color that it was quite startling.

"Oh, isn't it thrilling?" I gasped, and I almost forgot, for a while, all thoughts of Ifor and our next meeting.

"And it's only Monday," Gwenfron marveled. "It's only beginning. Tomorrow far more singers and dancers will be arriving."

We pushed our way through the crowd outside the station, hearing a mixture of languages, some of them unidentifiable. The rather sober-looking members of a Dutch choir went off in a motor coach to a village farther up the Dee. A number of Austrian dancers began to perform in a cleared space, looking as fresh and cheerful as though they had not just traveled straight through from Innsbruck.

It was utterly fascinating, and it was with difficulty that we tore ourselves away at half past eight. The Swiss dancers had not yet arrived, but they were expected any time, when they would be sent on to Nant Gwyncefn by coach. I had to be there to welcome my eight, so Gwenfron and I parted in the village, and I rode home rapidly to put on big kettles and to see that the meal was quite ready. They would probably be ravenously hungry.

It was a dream of an evening, and I wandered out restlessly into the ruins. I was sitting on a sun-warmed stone, trying not to go over that brief episode with Ifor for about the twelfth time, when I heard the sound of distant singing and laughter. Then an engine started up and I heard a large vehicle coming along the lane.

My Swiss were eight smiling young women in Bernese national costume; the last to be delivered. Their menfolk were at the post office, the inn, and some of the cottages. They tumbled out of the bus, dragging suitcases after them, and one of the Eisteddfod organizers read their names from a list. I caught several Christian names— Verena, Elsa, Klara, Anna, and we all smiled and smiled and shook hands over and over again.

They seemed immensely struck by the Priory ruins and began to spread all over the garth, staring and exclaiming. I thought fleetingly of Millicent, wondering what she would say. I felt that I had traveled very far from the Catrin Drury who had lived at home in Sloane Street, answerable to Millicent all the time.

Two of the Swiss, it seemed, could speak quite a lot of English, and they told me how happy they were to come to Wales and to find themselves staying in such an interesting place. I had quite a job to get them all indoors, but eventually they all knew their rooms and there was a great deal of laughter drifting down the tower stairs.

Presently they flocked in to supper, and my slight anxiety that they might not like the food I had prepared soon faded. They ate everything with apparent gusto, saying *"Gut! Gut!"* every time I passed a dish, and we all smiled a lot more and exchanged what information we could. They came from a very remote village in the Bernese Oberland, and this was their first visit to Britain. Patently they were out to enjoy themselves, but by the end of supper they were nearly all yawning, and one of the English-speakers said:

"We travel all night . . . we sit up in ze train, so stiff. Not comfortable. Such soft beds you got."

They insisted on helping me to clear away and wash up, and then, carrying jugs of hot water, went off to the soft beds, and I eventually reached mine, dead tired but very wakeful in spite of it.

It had been quite a day. So many things had happened, and Ifor . . . I tried not to think of him, but his face was clear in my mind as I drifted off to sleep at last.

Enchanted evening

And so the Eisteddfod began, or, more truly, it began with the concert the next evening, to which I went with Mrs. Williams and Gwenfron. The great marquee was banked with wonderful flowers, as Gwenfron had said it would be, and it was both exciting and moving to be there at the start of the Eisteddfod. My mind was already filled with colorful pictures after the long, sunny day: my Swiss girls and their partners dancing out on the garth, practicing for the morrow; foreign women sitting like exotic flowers on the black rocks of the Dee, singing and laughing; flags and dancing in the streets, and innumerable alien voices.

I had thought I ought to stay at the Priory, but my visitors went off into town at eleven, saying that they would be away until after the evening concert, and so I was really free, since the Society allowed me to close the

Priory at my discretion. It was the town that would attract everyone that day, not the end of a remote valley.

So the day passed, and at last I sat with Gwenfron and her mother in the marquee, while the great and famous orchestra tuned up and thousands upon thousands of people massed behind us. I was in Wales, in Llangollen, and I should have been happy, but I was not. I felt most unusually desolate, though I tried to hide it from my companions and myself.

The beautiful music did nothing to dispell my mood. Rather it increased it tenfold, and at last I was forced to tell myself that I was a fool to let the opening of the Eisteddfod be spoiled because Ifor was away in London and I was strangely lonely. Somehow it was all the worse because of our last brief meeting, because of the kiss and the words I still half believed I had imagined. I wanted to see Ifor again, and yet I was afraid. If he *had* said those words and meant them, it was the most wonderful thing that had ever happened to me. I knew now, with a painful, sharp awareness, that I, certainly, was in love.

By the next morning, however, I was more myself, for there was so little time for thought. I went into town in the bus with my Swiss visitors and was in the marquee well before nine o'clock, when the proceedings opened with a prayer, a hymn, and a penillion song with a harp. Gwenfron joined me just as the first team, a Danish one, appeared on the stage, and after that I was lost—completely and utterly—in the mounting color and excitement, the music and the movement.

It was breath-taking, somehow enhanced by that vast, pressing crowd. The Spanish dancing almost made my hair rise on my scalp, it was so exciting—the brilliant skirts of the women, the clicking of the castanets, the flamenco singing. And the Jugoslavs—a group, I had heard, that had visited Wales on many other occasions and often carried off the prizes—were like nothing I had ever seen, their dances so old and queer and strangely primitive, and they moved like one person, as though it was the most natural thing in the world to create that ancient, compelling rhythm.

There was a beautiful Scottish team, the men in kilts and the women in long white dresses with tartan sashes, but even to my ignorant eyes their elegant dancing was more that of the ballroom than purely folk dancing. But the audience loved them, and, in sharp contrast, they also loved the Swiss dancers, who looked so simple and gay. I was delighted about that, for naturally I felt a proprietary interest in them.

The marquee grew hotter and hotter, and more and more people crowded into the back, standing tightly packed in the aisles. Presently the attendants rolled up the sides of the vast tent so that one could see the green slopes of the hills, faintly dimmed in the heat haze.

Team followed team, each more fascinating than the last, and I was quite exhausted with heat and excitement and innumerable impressions when at last Gwenfron and I emerged into the open air, to sit on a dusty bank to eat our picnic lunch.

"I've never seen anything like it!" I cried. "The choirs will seem dull after this. But I still curl up at the thought of having to stand on that stage!"

"I shouldn't worry," Gwenfron said cheerfully. "We're on early, so we'll get it over. By the way, Ifor's coming home this evening. I knew he would."

And somehow, for all its wonder and gaiety, the Eisteddfod seemed less important after that.

The Swiss dancers placed third, and the judges said some very nice things about them. I was delighted, and so were Verena, Elsa, Anna, and the rest. They surrounded me on the Eisteddfod ground and chattered in a peculiar mixture of English and what seemed to be their valley dialect. It certainly wasn't ordinary German. Out of it emerged the fact that they wanted to ask some of the other groups to visit the Priory after the concert that night.

"Eet will be well?" Verena asked anxiously. "Not in ze ruin church, no. But on ze grass before ze 'ouse."

"Yes, of course, do," I said, smiling at them all. "But what about food and drink?"

They would see to all that, I was assured with many smiles and nods and eager gestures.

And so the long day and evening passed, a feast of foreign dancing and singing. And when we emerged from the evening concert the sky was stained rose and gold and the moon hung over the hills.

I had forgotten tiredness long before and was quite prepared to stay up all night. Gwenfron said the same, but pointed out prudently that we had to be fresh for the choir. She came back with us in the coach, and it was like a dream as we drove along the shadowed lanes.

The Priory looked beautiful in the sharp black and white of the night, and the air was so still and warm that not even a coat was necessary.

It seemed that nearly everyone staying in the valley had been asked to visit the Priory, and the garth was soon packed with Germans, Swiss, and Italians. There were accordionists, a man with a fiddle, and even a very old man with a long, long alphorn. He sat on a stone against the chapter-house wall, with the alphorn beside him, and I wondered if he felt very alien in the Welsh valley, among the little hills.

One might have thought that they had all done enough for one day, but not a bit of it. They were ready to try to learn each other's songs and dances, and Gwenfron and I found ourselves joining in as best we could. Gwenfron was with a handsome, smiling Italian and I with a charming young man from Berne, one of the yodelers.

It was all like a dream, and I felt strangely unlike myself, lost in pleasure in the moonlit scene and the warmth of international friendship.

I had forgotten Ifor, and then, suddenly, I turned around and saw him by the gate. For a moment I thought it a trick of the moonlight, but no, it really was Ifor!

As I looked across at him he beckoned, smiling, and I went slowly toward him, shy and uncertain. He had changed from town clothes to country ones and looked very tall in the shadows by the gate.

He put his hand on my arm briefly and said:

"Will you come up onto the hills, Catrin?"

"But it's long after midnight," I said with a little gasp. "And I suppose I'm the hostess——"

"They don't need you, and time doesn't seem to matter tonight." Then somehow we were walking together down the lane, under the dark trees, and up the rather rougher track to the top of the hills, where we had met that very first time in the hail shower. As we climbed we said little; there seemed no need for words. The moonlit night wrapped us round, warm and still and sweet-smelling.

High on the hills, we stood and looked down at the Priory, the arches just faintly visible among the trees. The sound of music and laughter and voices came up to us, and then suddenly there was a hush.

Out of the night came the long deep note of the horn, rising and falling in a way that went straight to my heart. So rich and strange—a sound that was meant for a high Alpine valley, striking echoes of deep sound from snow-covered mountain peaks.

Ifor and I stood close together in the bracken, and, as the sound of the alphorn died away, the yodeling began. And after that the wonderful singing of the male choir from Milan. They were too distant for us to recognize the language, and yet I knew it was the Italians.

The sound rose and rose, filling the quiet valley, and I thought, so deeply moved that I would have been afraid to speak, that this was the real concert—not that one in the hot marquee.

I had forgotten shyness and doubt, and when Ifor said, "Come and sit on that rock, Catrin," I went willingly, still a little dazed, but warm and happy. And of course, as I had known since I had seen Ifor by the gate, I had not imagined any of it.

"You will marry me, Catrin?" Ifor asked after a little while, and I answered:

"Yes. Oh, yes. But I'm only eighteen. What shall we do if Father and Millicent won't agree?"

"So very young!" Ifor said, laughing. "But plenty of girls are married at eighteen. Only, Catrin, I don't want to stop you from doing the things you had planned, unless —— Well, unless you're quite sure."

"I am sure," I told him. "I don't think I'm the sort of girl to care much about a career. There isn't anything I do especially well. It must be different, there must be some pull, if one has special talents, like dancing or acting. Or like Gwenfron, caring so much about training to be a nurse. I love Nant Gwyncefn and the farm. I—I was dreading going away forever. But what about your mother? Oh, Ifor, how will she feel? And Gwenfron?"

"Gwenfron will be delighted," he said firmly. "She always wished she had a sister. And Mother will be pleased, too. She likes you, Catrin. Once everything is settled I think she'll probably go to Canada for a long visit. She always said she'd feel free when I married." And then we cast aside plans and questions and lost ourselves in the magic of the moment.

When, at last, we came down the hill road, everyone was going home up the valley, singing, and that enchanted time was nearly over.

Catrin looks back

Now it's September and I'm back in Sloane Street. The Eisteddfod seems much more than two months ago—that lovely, gay time that will come back another year. I actually enjoyed singing in the Gwyncefn choir, and we got a high rating, though we didn't win a prize.

Aunt Mair returned to the Priory at the end of July, and her old friend from Llanrwst came to spend a few weeks with her. I stayed on for a week or two and then returned to London, and Ifor traveled with me, to see Father and Millicent.

Father liked him at once, I knew that, but Millicent was not so sure. I think she was suspicious of him because he was a Welshman and a playwright, but she didn't say very much.

"You'll go your own way, no doubt, Catrin," she said to me when Ifor had gone. "But I don't see why you can't wait until you meet a pleasant young man who lives in

London. Burying yourself in that lonely valley—being a farmer's wife—surrounded by Welsh-speaking people——"

"But I shan't really be 'buried,' " I said. I felt much more assured with Millicent than I had been before. "Ifor will be in London quite a lot, and the new manager will look after the farm."

"Wait until you have children," she said. "Then there won't be so much gadding about. How will you feel about that?"

Well, I wasn't going to tell Millicent, of all people, exactly how I felt about it, so I merely said cheerfully:

"I don't think I shall mind. I really do love Nant Gwyncefn, and I'm not even afraid of the depths of winter. And there'll be Gwenfron. She'll come home whenever she can. Chester isn't very far away. Don't worry, Millicent. I shall be happy."

"I see you will," she said with a quick, almost rueful glance. "And evidently your father sees it, too."

Father did see it. He kissed me and said:

"Well, you're young. I would have preferred you to wait until you're twenty-one, but I know it's no use arguing. And since Penelope isn't coming back from Paris, you couldn't have shared an apartment with her. You have all my blessings, Catrin, and I know that your mother would have been very happy to think of you marrying a Welshman."

So that was that, and the wedding was fixed for the first of October, in London. That is nearly a month off, and I am very busy. Delphine is going to be my bridesmaid, and a little boy cousin on Father's side of the family will be a very charming page. I wanted Gwenfron, but she has just started nursing and will not be able to have enough time off to come to London. She is sorry, and so am I, but she seems very happy with her work, though she says she is so tired each night that she just flops into bed and knows nothing more until work begins the next day. Aunt Mair is coming to my wedding, though; she is going to stay here in Sloane Street.

Millicent has really turned out much more sympathetic than I expected, and she is helping me with all my shopping and plans.

Last night was Ifor's first night—the first night of *Penillion for David Evans*. Father, Millicent, Mrs. Williams, Ifor, and I were all in one of the stage boxes, and it was both exciting and terrifying; terrifying in case the critics didn't like the play. But by the end of the second act I had almost ceased to care; or, rather, I was so lost in the play that I could not doubt that they were lost, too. Sometimes I looked at Ifor with a sense of incredulity. He had created the play, and, during it, he looked so dark and remote.

Then afterward, when he went on stage, he was smiling and looked happy, and everyone clapped and clapped, and we were all pretty sure that *Penillion* was going to be an even greater success than *Death of the Dragon*.

Later still we had supper at the Savoy, and even Millicent melted, though I knew she had not cared for the play.

"Well, you're a lucky girl, I suppose," she murmured to me. "He's evidently well on the way toward being a success. It's not as though he's an ordinary farmer."

I have just read every newspaper I can lay hands on, and most of the critics liked the play. Some even say that it will be transferred to another theater after its six weeks at the Royal Crown, and they prophesy a record run.

I'm delighted for Ifor's sake, but my mind keeps going back to Nant Gwyncefn, to the farmhouse on the hillside, the bracken turning golden all over the slopes, and the stubble fields pale and quiet on either side of the little river.

I love Ifor and I love Nant Gwyncefn. I shall love it in snow and winter cold. So it was certainly the most important thing I ever did in my life when I pulled the Priory bell that day at the beginning of May. How long ago it seems!